Also by Erin Downing

Drive Me Crazy

Prom Crashers

Dancing Queen

KISS IT

ERIN DOWNING

Simon Pulse
New York London Toronto Sydney

SIMON PULSE

An imprint of Simon & Schuster Children's Publishing Division

1230 Avenue of the Americas, New York, NY 10020

First Simon Pulse paperback edition June 2010

Copyright © 2010 by Erin Soderberg Downing

All rights reserved, including the right of reproduction in whole or in part in any form.

SIMON PULSE and colophon are registered trademarks of Simon & Schuster, Inc.

For information about special discounts for bulk purchases, please contact Simon & Schuster Special Sales at 1-866-506-1949 or business@simonandschuster.com.

The Simon & Schuster Speakers Bureau can bring authors to your live event. For more information or to book an event contact the Simon & Schuster Speakers Bureau at 1-866-248-3049 or visit our website at www.simonspeakers.com.

Designed by Mike Rosamilia

The text of this book was set in Adobe Caslon Pro.

Manufactured in the United States of America

2 4 6 8 10 9 7 5 3

Library of Congress Cataloging-in-Publication Data

Downing, Erin.

Kiss it / by Erin Downing.

p. cm.

Summary: Small-town Minnesotan Chastity (Chaz) Bryan wants nothing more than to get some sexual experience before she graduates from high school and moves away, but when she meets an intriguing boy visiting from North Carolina over Christmas break, her tough-girl facade slowly breaks down.

ISBN 978-1-4169-9700-9 (pbk)

[1. Self-realization—Fiction. 2. Interpersonal relations—Fiction. 3. Sex—Fiction. 4. Secrets—Fiction. 5. Family life—Minnesota—Fiction. 6. Minnesota—Fiction.]

I. Title.

PZ7.D759273Ki 2010

[Fic]—dc22

2009036507

ISBN 978-1-4169-9701-6 (eBook)

This one's for me.

PROLOGUE

THE TV SCREEN GLOWED PINK IN basement darkness. An animalistic squeal echoed out of the surround-sound system my dad had installed as an early Christmas gift for himself. The squealing became grunts, pulsing from the speaker that shared shelf space with a gilt-framed photo of my grandma Nonna. Her rosary was hanging off one corner of the frame.

Two rabbits (oblivious to the voyeur who was lurking in the shadows, taping their carnal pleasure for future analysis on Animal Planet) humped with reckless abandon. Their speed and ferocity made clear their single-minded objective: Get laid, as quickly and as often as possible.

Never mind the fact that you'll have a litter of bunnies in a month, I thought. *Fuck for fuck's sake.*

If only it were that simple for the rest of us.

**1.** **"I'M TURNING THIS OFF." MY BEST**
friend, Sadie, furrowed her precious brow, squinching up her
eyes to hide from the vulgarity on the TV screen. She grabbed
the remote from my hands and silenced the *thump-thump* of
animal mating. "This is sick, Chaz. You're sick for making me
watch it."

In fact she was right. I, Chastity Bryan, am nothing if
not a total perv. It has been this way since I first squeezed
my tiny ta-tas into that beginner bra back in seventh grade.
My parents are perfectly respectable people, churchgoers and

community leaders, yadda yadda. But their daughter—me—inherited some sort of nasty gene, and I am magnetically drawn to all things sexual rather than all things traditionally considered "Minnesota nice." "It's nature, Sade. Humans do it too, you know."

She glared at me. "It's sick, Chaz. Who watches bunnies making love?"

"What they were doing is called 'humping.' Plain and simple." I shrugged, as though sex were a regular, daily activity for me. As if.

As if I'd ever *really* done it.

As if there were anyone in my town worth doing it with.

As if I would ever get laid.

Unfortunately, I was born in Milton, Minnesota, where the options for sinful human sexuality involve screwing a guy named Vic who drives a snowmobile to school or taking advantage of a scrawny twerp like Herbie Landon. You don't know Herbie Landon, but you know guys like him. He's decorated with ready-to-pop backne and hairless legs that shake around inside his jeans like chicken bones. Super hot, right?

Bottom line: I'd had something that resembled sex (I liked to believe what I'd done was "distantly related to the sex family"), but I'd never gotten laid in any kind of real way. I talked a big game and acted like an expert in doing the nasty, but I was as sexless as a deflated blow-up doll. Therefore I got the sexual tension out of my system verbally.

"Don't you feel guilty, talking like that in front of your grandma?" I looked over at the picture of Nonna. My grandma's eyebrow was lifted, as if to prove Sadie's point. Whatever. Nonna had been a fireball back in her day, of that I was certain. I got my vulgarity and honesty from someone, and that someone certainly wasn't my mom. Mom and I are more like oil and water than yin and yang—we don't see eye to eye on much of anything, and we certainly don't complement each other. We couldn't be more different.

"Nonna loves it," I mused. "And PS, it's not as if she can hear anything we're saying."

Sadie pursed her lips. "She can hear you from heaven, Chaz. And she's frowning down upon you, worried about the young woman you've become." Sadie delivered this sermon seriously, but it was just a lecture for the sake of lecturing. Her ranting rolled off my back like hot chocolate sauce.

"I'm a lovely young woman, according to Mrs. Vos and the Academic Achievement Committee." I shifted on the couch and took control of the remote again, pushing the on button.

"Mrs. Vos is blind in one eye and doesn't leave the library," Sadie replied. That was true. "Besides, our whole class probably thinks you're a lovely young woman. No one knows you like I do, Chastity Bryan. You actually seem sort of normal—blandly normal."

I grinned. "That's my goal." It was, actually. Blending in and keeping up appearances are everything in a small town like Milton. I was already the odd one out in my family, and that was hard enough. I only needed to suffer through this charade for six more months; then I would be out of this house and this town going . . . somewhere else. With different people. The specifics were still to be determined.

"You'd think after living eighteen years in Milton, someone besides me would know the real you." Sadie shook her head. When she said the next bit, I knew she was being silly, but it struck an honest chord and, quite frankly, stung a little. "No boyfriends, no scandal, no dirt. It's like you never even existed in this town."

That was the point.

"Ugh, I feel terrible," Sadie muttered. I peeked out from behind the shower curtain and spotted Sades assessing her flawless forehead in my mom's ultramagnifying facial mirror.

We had hung out in the basement, channel-surfing, for a little while longer, until I reluctantly hit the shower to prepare myself for work at Matt's Bar, our town dive and my humble place of employment. Sadie was keeping me company, but mostly she was hanging in the bathroom so she could be near the toilet. She'd eaten something nasty at her cousin's house the weekend before, and ever since she'd been lingering near the loo.

"Isn't a stomach virus supposed to go away in, like, twenty-four hours?" she whined.

"You've gotta let it slink through your system and take its own sweet time."

"Doesn't your shift start at six?" Sadie asked, after a pause during which I was sure she was popping an unseen zit.

I turned the water off and grabbed my towel from its hook. "Yeah," I admitted. "I'm running a little late."

"It's six now."

"I get it."

"I can get a ride with you, right?" Sadie asked.

"I just assumed that's why you were still here."

She grinned. "I'm meeting Trav at Matt's. He can give me a ride home."

"Ooh." My voice came out furry from under my towel. I had my head flipped upside down to dry my tangled mess of brown curls. "Sneaking out with the boy without Mom knowing, huh? Am I your alibi?"

Looking out from under my mass of knotted hair, I saw

Sadie open her wide blue eyes guiltily. "Are you okay with that?" she asked earnestly.

"Sade, have I ever judged?" I stepped naked out of the shower stall, my towel a turban. "I like to be your alibi. I appreciate the fact that at least you're getting some. One of us should be having sex. Of course, it should be me, since you seem so crippled with guilt about it, but whatever."

Sadie dropped her head, groaning. I could sense the vomit boiling up again, and I hustled out of the bathroom and down the hall to my room. My parents were at a church dinner or something, so the nudity mattered not.

I held my boobs as I sauntered into my room, cupping them inside my warm palms. I'm proud of my tits, but a little dismayed that they don't spill out from between my fingers when I grab them like this. Sadie's boobs are Cs—in some brands Ds, even—and I always envy her for how she looks in snug-fitting T-shirts. I have runner legs, though, and know that what I lack in chest volume I make up for in skinny legs that actually look good in cheap jeans.

I grabbed a boring bra out of my drawer, strapping my little guys in under two thin triangular swatches of pink fabric. Then I threw on my Matt's Bar T-shirt and a pair of baggy jeans and headed back down the hall to the bathroom. Peering around the partly closed door, I called, "You okay?"

"How much of this crap is in me?" Sadie moaned as she passed a comb out the crack of open door. I took the hint, pulling the cheap plastic through my thick, unruly mane.

"Ready to go?"

"Are *you*?" Sadie opened the door to give me the once-over. "Your hair is half brushed."

"It's Matt's," I replied. "That's good enough."

And then we took off.

Matt's Bar is on the main street in town, wedged between the gas station and an old, run-down movie theater. We don't get first-run films in Milton anymore. The theater was once a second-run discount theater, then an indie-film venue, and now it's an adult-movie place. Sadie lives less than a half mile away from Matt's, still technically "in town," but I live a few miles down a dirt road, literally on the outskirts of nowhere.

I pulled into the lot behind the bar and went through the back door. Sadie tentatively followed—she gets a little weird about coming into Matt's without her parents, since it's called a bar and all, but really, Matt's is just a regular old restaurant with a few old drunks who frequent the place. You can't afford to be picky in Milton, since Matt's is one of three options for eating out.

Gina's Pizza, which is owned by Matt's ex-wife, is down at

the other end of town and serves up more health-code viola-
tions than slices. Then there's Café Cheapo (it's officially Café
Français, but I'm not sure anyone even knows that), which
sells these nasty sandwiches and burned cappuccinos. Dining
is not a highlight in Milton—you have to drive twenty miles
to Flanders, population fifteen thousand, if you want to get
McDonald's or a piece of steak.

In truth Matt's actually has decent food. We're sort of
famous for our cheeseburgers, and the fries are cooked in bacon
grease that drips off the racks above the fryers. That sounds
totally grode, but people like it, and that means business is
steady most of the time. Matt also had a fling with a Jamaican
chick years ago, so we serve a yummy jerk chicken that people
even drive in from Minneapolis for every now and then.

"Are you cool?" I asked Sadie as I ducked under the counter. "Sit—I'll get you a root beer."

For a Saturday night the place was pretty slow. There were
only a few tables full, and it looked like Angela had already
waited on all of them. "You're late," Angela chirped, pecking
me on the cheek as she hustled by with two handfuls of empty
pint glasses.

"Sorry."

"I don't care—Matt's in back, and I covered for you. Pay
me back by having us all over next weekend?"

I rolled my eyes. "Yeah, whatever." The crew from Matt's loves coming to my house, since the basement is big and now has surround-sound HDTV, and my parents leave us pretty much alone. Angela graduated from high school a year ago and should have her own place, but she still lives with her parents in a tiny little house at the very edge of town. She needs to get out of there, but who am I to judge?

"Thanks, babe." Angela beamed as she flitted by, off to the kitchen to unload the dirty glasses. And probably sneak in a little kissy-kissy with Ryan the dishwasher, who she's been hanging out with lately. "Oh, and you're on table six. You're welcome!"

I glanced over at the table nearest the front window—guy, late teens/early twenties, alone. "Thank you," I muttered to Angela, who was long gone. I pulled my lip gloss out of my pocket and strolled over to my first table of the night. "Any questions?" I asked, hands on hips. The guy sitting at the table looked up, and my heart thudded nervously.

"What do you recommend?" He had been squinting to read the menu, and his eyes stayed bunched up when he looked at me. There was something very James Dean about his look that made me feel a little dangerous all of a sudden. Of course, his puffy black Patagonia jacket was totally nonrugged, but the look on his face made me think he was up to no good most of the time. I was probably inventing this for my own sexual fantasy, but I wanted to believe I was right.

I blinked deliberately, the flirt instinct kicking into gear. This guy was *not* from around here, and I had to do my part to make him stay.

Milton needed a guy like this.

I needed a guy like this.

I lowered my lashes and sucked my pen. "The cheeseburger is famous. But if you haven't had jerk chicken . . ."

"What do *you* like?" he asked. His lips curled into a smirk. It may have been his natural look, but I imagined the expression had been crafted just for me.

I shrugged. "It's your call. I like it all."

"Really?" He leaned back in his chair and dropped the menu back into its slot in between the ketchup and mustard in the middle of the table. "Surprise me."

He knew he was hot. Of that I was certain. I looked at him for one more second, then turned on my heel and walked away. "I want that guy," I declared to Sadie as I returned to the bar. "I *must have* that guy." She turned one hundred eighty degrees in her seat and stared at the sexpot at table six. "Nice. Thanks for the subtlety, Sade."

"Who is he?"

"No clue," I responded, writing up a ticket for a cheeseburger, fries, and a side of jerk chicken. If table six was going to be coy about it, I might as well give him a big order and hope he tipped 20 percent. I slapped the ticket up on the counter between the bar and the kitchen and called, "Order in!" to Wolf, the cook.

"He wasn't in Jeremy's class." She watched my boy from her post at the bar. Jeremy is Sadie's brother. He graduated from Milton two years ago and moved far, far away to Flanders. Flanders is a popular postgraduation destination for Milton High alums. The thought of that being my future horrifies me. It simply will not happen.

I shook my head and took a sip of water through a straw. "That guy is not from Milton," I declared. "That *jacket* is not from Milton." I watched the front door ease open and saw Trav peek in. "Trav's here."

Sadie instantly perked up, her postpuke face flushing pink again. "Thanks for the lift, Chastity." She hopped off her bar stool and bundled up inside her thick, furry parka. "See ya Monday at school, 'kay?"

I cringed at the sound of my full name, then waved them out of the bar. "Be safe!" But Sadie was already gone—as if they needed the warning anyway.

"Order up!" Wolf peered up over the kitchen window. "What up, Chaz?" With his tongue he pushed a wad of chew back into place inside his cheek. In case you were wondering, Wolf is his real name. Wolf's brother is Bear, and his dad goes by Skunk. The mom is long gone. Do you blame her?

"Thanks." The plate was hot, but it didn't really affect me. I'm tough as nails, a waitress extraordinaire. When I got to his table, Sexy Boy was texting someone. I lingered until he hit send.

He looked up at me expectantly, pulling gum out of his mouth to stuff it in the corner of his napkin. "Did you want some? You ordered me enough to feed both of us."

I shrugged. "Is that a real offer? If so, yeah."

"Sit."

My mind flashed ahead to a future scene where he would grab me and throw me down on a bed or a couch or a floor (I wasn't picky), commanding me with the same voice he'd just used for the word "sit." I wanted that scene to happen. Now. "Do you like?" I wrapped my fingers around the neck of the ketchup bottle and settled into the seat across from him to grab a fry.

When he answered, "God, yes," his mouth was full of cheesy burger, and a tiny piece of toasted bun was stuck in his intentionally overgrown facial hair. I reached out and grabbed the crumb. Again, the flash of future sex scenes danced in my head, and my tongue licked my lips instinctively. His lips were a little on the thin side, but they looked like the perfect dessert nonetheless.

Oh, God, I thought. *I need this guy.* Though I wanted to get up and sit on his lap, I chose instead to say, "You're not from here." He looked up, lifting an eyebrow. "There are three thousand people in Milton, and our high school graduating class is thirty-five. Thirty-four if you take out Melinda Planton, who skipped too many days to graduate. Let's just say I think I know most people my age."

"And what age is that?" he asked.

I popped a fry into my mouth, chewed, then finally said, "Eighteen."

He smiled, a trickle of grease illuminating the edge of his lower lip. "Same."

"Great."

A pause, then he admitted, "I live in North Carolina."

"Why the hell are you here?"

"Are you the welcoming committee?"

I laughed at that. *I'd like to welcome him, all right.* "It just seems like a long way from home. And Milton is sort of a random stop for someone visiting Minnesota."

"My dad moved here last summer. Chris Bowman?"

"The guy who runs the wilderness outfitter?" I could picture him—but he was still new to town and didn't get an invite to my folks' holiday party, so I didn't know him or anything.

He nodded. "Custody battle. My dad won Christmas break this year, so he and my mom decided to give me a bonus week of winter break to spend quality time here in the Great North Woods with Dad."

"Nice. Lucky you." As I led a forkful of chicken toward my mouth, I noticed Matt watching me from behind the bar. "Enjoy, okay?" I got up and sashayed back to the bar.

When I dropped the check on his table a little while later, the North Carolina hottie grabbed my arm. "Don't waitresses usually sign the check? Write something like, 'Thanks, heart, Deanna?'"

"I don't do that." I relished the feeling of his fingers on me. *Touch me everywhere,* I begged (silently).

"You should. That way I'd know your name."

"You could just ask me, you know."

"Okay."

"Okay?" I asked, teasing him. If by touching me he could play with my physical senses the way he was, I could fuck with his mind a little bit, right?

"I'm Sebastian." Pause. "So?" He looked at me expectantly, the squint back in his eyes. "What's your name?"

"Chastity."

He smiled and asked nothing more.

When he left a few minutes later, I was in back, trying to breathe again.

He tipped 40 percent.

Angela stopped me on my way out after my shift. She and Wolf were smoking out back next to the Dumpster—Matt would be closing up soon, and the place was empty. Angela took a drag on her cigarette and blew it in my general direction. It was bitterly cold outside—if I'd smoked, I'd sure as hell have quit in this weather. "You're gonna screw that guy, aren't you?" Angela said gleefully.

"Ange, that is the goal."

Wolf chuckled, shaking his head. "Your first kiss, huh? You really want to lose it to Mr. Patagonia?"

"What?" I said, all innocence. "You think I'm saving myself for you?" I narrowed my eyes at Wolf. "Let's see . . . scrawny legs, chew pack, rotted-out teeth, and a penis the size of a French fry? Oh, I'm dreaming of the day." Ange cracked up— she'd hooked up with Wolf, and I'd been treated to the sordid details. *All* of the miniscule detail.

"I'm gonna get that cherry, Chaz." Wolf was amusing himself. "You know you want it, baby." He spat a slimy chew loogie at the base of the Dumpster. It slid down the cold metal and pooled into a pile of rapidly freezing goober on the asphalt.

"Kiss it, freak," I replied, touching my lips to my middle finger before flashing it at him. "My cherry was plucked long ago, and it was sex that would rock your world." Then I hopped in my car and peeled out of the Matt's lot as fast as my little Toyota would let me.

**2.** **I'D LIED TO WOLF. MY "CHERRY**
plucking" had been about as thrilling as a visit to the SPAM
processing plant in Austin, Minnesota. It had happened
almost exactly a year ago, and I was still paying the conse-
quences of my actions. Not with scabies or a baby or emotional scarring or anything as dramatic as that. No, my
actions were haunting me in the form of romantic obsession
by the dopey Hunter Johnson. And romance and touchy-
feely bullshit were not things I needed—then, or ever.

Here's how it all went down:

It was Saturday afternoon, the first day of winter break. My parents were gearing up for their annual *kladdkaka* and *köttbullar* holiday party. That means gooey chocolate cake and meatballs, to translate it for the non-Swedes (my mom's maiden name is Ingvarsson, in case you were wondering where the Swedish connection came from). My folks host this little festival every year, and damn near everyone in our rinky-dink town comes over for spiced rum punch (called *glögg* in Svenska) and awkward mingling.

Things only get interesting after someone—usually Mrs. Krapp—accidentally flashes a tit or says someone's wife looks a little thicker around the middle. The best was the time James Livingston accidentally dropped his keys into the bowl of pickled herring slices, and Mrs. Krapp fished them out with her mouth. Granted, that happened after the party had been swinging for, like, seven hours, and there were only a few drunken stragglers left, but it was classic.

Mrs. Krapp was in the hospital for some unknown ailment (probably cirrhosis) during last year's party, which meant it was a little milder than usual. So I ended up spicing things up with a little fun of my own design.

For years my mom had been harping on about the quality and potential of Hunter Johnson. She and Miriam Johnson are in church choir together, and apparently they do a lot more gabbing than singing in choir practice. She knows weird things about Hunter that I don't care to know.

Such as, he was at one time prone to flaky scalp. He started using some special Internet-order shampoo, which gave him thick, lustrous locks that my mom is very fond of. I knew this because my mom came home recommending the shampoo to me after I'd complained about my hair being lifeless and dull.

"He's such a nice kid," my mom said once, after we'd bumped into Hunter at the car wash/gas station where he works on weekends. "You can't do much better than that."

"Wow. Thanks, Mom."

My mom rolled her eyes at me in the rearview mirror. I always sit in back when I ride around town with my mom. She's taken the new car seat regulations to the extreme and is convinced that I am safest in the back, never mind the fact that I'm eighteen and have my driver's license. I don't mind her little neuroses—it makes me more comfortable to keep my distance. With her up front and me behind, I can also pretend that she is my driver and put a pretend plastic shield (à la cop cars) between us. Imagination is a useful tool every now and again. That's all I have in my rural hell of a hometown.

After Mom glared at me in the mirror, she stopped to smooth her eyebrows into a tidy line. "You know what I mean—Hunter is a catch."

"If you don't mind, I'll politely disagree," I replied. As if knowing that Hunter had dandruff was going to win me over. As if I'd ever take my mom's recommendation on a guy. *Ick*.

She fixed me with a look, her manicured brows arched into little peaks. "It's never polite to disagree with your mother." She returned her eyes to the road.

"To that I will politely disagree once more. A girl needs to learn to stand up for herself, or she'll simply become the next victim of domestic assault and corporate discrimination."

My mom released an icy breath from between pinched lips. I knew it was cool and wintergreen-scented because I'd just seen her pop four mini breath mints into her mouth. Besides which, everything my mom said was downright chilly. "Why are you so dramatic and strange?" she demanded.

"Strange" does not equal "good" in my mom's view. Conformity and normalcy and keeping things at a distance are far preferable. "I'm just saying, I'm not interested in Hunter Johnson. He's totally boring."

"You'll come around," she reasoned. "You'll see."

The conversation had ended there that day, but it picked up again very shortly thereafter at the holiday party. Just as last year's party was swinging into gear, my mom proudly announced that Miriam Johnson was bringing her son, my classmate. I stuffed my mouth with meatballs and hoped to choke just enough that I'd be excused for the night. Instead I drooled sauce and spent the rest of the party wearing a shirt with a greasy splat.

When Hunter arrived, sporting a stunning green button-down dress shirt and a red cardigan, I strolled over and murmured, "That sweater is hot."

Hunter's face lit up like a furnace, his cheeks a splotchy red pattern that glowed with embarrassment. "It's a holiday theme," he explained. "Red and green, you know?"

"I get it, Hunter." He was so awkward. "Do you want some punch?"

His eyes brightened, looking toward the well-stocked buffet and bar. The booze-free punch bowl was right next to the festive variety, and I could tell that Hunter and I were on the same page. "Should I get two?" he offered.

"Please." When he returned with our hot, toasty, drunken cups, Hunter and I sat together on the love seat in the living room. My mom and Miriam were all atwitter in the kitchen, stealing glances at us with hope bubbling up and out of every crevice. "I'm glad you came," I told Hunter honestly. I was so sick of playing nice at these parties, and my parents never let me hide away in my room alone. Apparently, not wanting to play with adults was antisocial, and no other kids were ever forced to come to these things.

I noticed for the first time that Hunter was a tiny bit cuter than I'd previously given him credit for. Perhaps the *glögg* had given me a nice pair of beer goggles—it certainly had armed me with a bonus boost of confidence. "Me too," Hunter said, eagerly gulping down a steaming glassful. "Thanks for asking your mom to ask mine if I would come."

"Pardon?" Was he nuts? Did he honestly think that I'd specifically requested his presence?

"My mom said you asked if I could—" He broke off, embarrassed. "You didn't, did you?"

"Um, no." I cringed. "I think our moms are obsessed with us hooking up." He reddened again. I so enjoy making boys squirm. All it takes is a little honesty and a few carefully selected words, and they are jelly. This could be fun. I set my half-full cup on the coffee table and switched over to a whisper. "Maybe we *should* just hook up and make them happy, huh?"

Hunter choked down the rest of his rum punch and looked at me like I was crazy. I just stared back. "Are you being serious?" he asked finally, pulling his sweater off and balling it up on his lap.

I let my hand drop to my side, and my fingers danced along the outside of his thigh before settling in under my own ass. "Interested?"

He blinked and stood up, holding his cardigan across the front of his body like a shield. I hopped off the couch and led the way toward the stairs to my room. As we passed my mom I said cheerfully, "We're going to go listen to some music."

Miriam beamed, and my mom responded, "Okeydokey." *Oh, parents. They're so sweet.*

Here's the thing: I'd obviously been wanting to get it on for quite some time, but opportunity just didn't knock all that often. In fact opportunity had never knocked for me, so I was pretty freaking eager to open that door while someone was standing on the other side.

Granted, Hunter wasn't exactly the charming, irresistible stallion I'd been hoping for, but I lacked the gene that makes a lot of girls feel like they need to lose it to someone special. I'd always seen the virginity handicap as a hurdle I simply needed to step over so that I could get on with my sexual liberation already. Based on his reaction, I figured Hunter was happy to play along. It wasn't like we would need to become soul mates afterward—we could just have a little fun.

I pulled Hunter into my bedroom and pushed him up against the door to close it behind us. His breath was coming in short, rum-scented bursts. In a surprisingly hot move Hunter grabbed my wrists and maneuvered me so I was up against the wall, his body pinning mine. "Is this okay?" he half moaned, clearly hoping for the answer I was about to give him.

I nodded and felt something hard poking through the thin fabric at the top of his jeans pocket. *Ooh, nice,* I mused. *That is one of the attributes my mom didn't use to sell Hunter.* His was not a small package. "We can go on the bed if you want."

He moaned again, which made me chuckle. "What's funny?" he pulled back, obviously self-conscious.

I answered by pulling him over to the bed. I lay down and looked up at him standing there framed against the dim twilight coming through the window. If I could get past the puffy hair and scrawny body, Hunter was actually kind of cute. Maybe ...?

He eased himself into a sitting position, then stood back up to take off his shoes, placing them side by side at the foot of my bed. He grinned sheepishly before lying down next to me, caressing my hair with his long fingers. It was a sweet gesture, but I really didn't want Hunter to get any wrong ideas. This was not the start of a relationship, and it was not a seduction scene. We were both in my room for one thing, and I for one was ready to get on with it.

I ran my left hand down the front of his body, stroking his stomach on my way to something else. Another groan—I held my laughter this time. My fingers reached for his fly, releasing the button before carefully pulling the zipper down. His pants flapped open, and I could see the bulge waiting to escape.

I could feel Hunter holding his breath, and his heart thumped wildly next to me. I chose not to look at him, for fear I would crack up. In truth I was a little nervous, this close to something I'd been curious about for so long. My nerves often came out as laughter.

My hand opened his pants farther, and two fingers slipped inside the buttoned flap of his boxers. I knew my hand was cold, and I had a momentary urge to apologize, but I was pretty sure it didn't really matter. He was hot inside his boxers, his skin firm and soft at the same time. My fingers started to do their own thing, rubbing upward and downward gently. Another moan.

I sat up on my knees and lifted one leg over his body. He adjusted himself so he was in the middle of my bed and I was straddled over him, both of us still mostly clothed. I slid down so I was over his thighs, then pulled his jeans down. His eyes were closed, and I was pretty sure he thought I was moving in for a blow job. That was *so* not going to happen—if we were going to do this, I wanted to get something out of it too, and no matter what girls say, giving a guy a blow is totally non-rewarding. And no guy is willing to reciprocate once you've done the deed. I learned that the not-so-fun way with Trent

Radnor, the last boy I'd been with, back in tenth grade.

Both of my hands moved to the top of Hunter's boxers, and I unfastened the button that held the fly closed. "Do you have any protection?" I asked quietly. I did, but I wanted to see if he was prepared for something like this. I guess it was a little game or something—if he'd said no, I would have given him a condom from my underwear drawer anyway. I wanted to see him squirm a little.

His eyes popped open. "Yeah," he said quickly, reaching for his wallet in the front pocket of his jeans. It took a little maneuvering, but he got it and pulled out a ratty-looking condom packet. It probably hadn't been in there for long, but I swapped it with a crisp, new one from my drawer. I knew mine had been treated properly and hadn't been melting in Hunter's wallet. I was on the pill, but a high-quality rubber was essential for my peace of mind. He ripped open the package, looking confused and amazed. "Are you sure you're okay with this?"

I smiled. "That's sweet of you." I meant it. "Yeah, I'm definitely okay with this."

He looked relieved. "Um, Chaz?"

"Yeah?" I had just straddled him and was beginning to unbutton my own jeans.

"I haven't done this before."

"That's okay," I promised. Then I pulled my zipper down

and slid my jeans and underwear past my hips and onto the floor. He lifted his head slightly to look at me, and I could feel him shudder beneath me. He left his boxers on and pulled his thing out of the little peephole to slide the condom on. I was definitely cool with this setup, since there was something less intimate about it that way—I liked the layer of fabric protection between our bodies.

Hunter was holding his breath again as he unrolled the condom. I moved into position, and he held himself straight up beneath me. It took a second of rearranging things, but we finally got lined up, and I lowered myself down onto him. Just as I started to feel the pinch that they warn you about with your first time, I felt him stiffen and saw him make a face that let me know the first time was over. Just like that.

Eyes squeezed shut, he held very still. After a few seconds he sheepishly peeked at me. "Oh," he muttered.

"Yep." I nodded, rolling off of him to lie on my back on the bed. I pulled my comforter up to cover myself. "Oh."

"I'm really sorry. I tried to hold it."

"But you couldn't, and now it's over," I said lightly. I wasn't trying to make him feel guilty or anything, but I certainly didn't want him to think this lame attempt at sex was going to count as something magnificent for me.

He pulled the condom off and wrapped it in a tissue from

my bedside table. He awkwardly held the messy tissue in his hand as he pulled his pants back up and buttoned them. He sat on the edge of the bed, looking frustratingly guilty and sated all at once. It was amusing, really. He clearly felt obligated to feel bad about his poor performance, but was overwhelmed by his immense pride at having had sex.

Me? Not as impressed with my first time. I was definitely ready to try that again, hopefully for more than four seconds next time. Ideally, with someone a little more interesting—and someone who wouldn't obsess about it for the next twelve months.

"You should probably get back downstairs," I said finally. "Your mom might come looking for you." I knew that would be enough to put the fear of God in him—I wanted him out of there. I was afraid if he lingered on, he would get the wrong idea that I was looking for something from him after letting him in my pants like that.

"Okay." He walked to the door, dumping the tissue-wrapped condom in my trash on his way across the room. *Ew.* "Hey, do you want to go out sometime?"

Though I felt guilty about it later, I didn't regret my response at the time: "Never, Hunter. Now get the fuck out."

That was almost a year ago. I could never tell if Hunter continued to harbor feelings for me because of the sex and his hope for more or because he was actually interested. He was too much of a chickenshit to tell me either way.

I would have probably been willing to let Hunter give it another go—he had the parts I was looking for, and the right proportion of good stuff at that. Miraculously, he'd opted against telling anyone at school about our little rendezvous, which helped his cause somewhat. But he had been acting like such a lovestruck loser since that party that I couldn't possibly let him back in there.

If he had been willing to just let the sex be, we could have tried again. But circumstances were such that I had to close the door, lock it, and put a fancy little eye-hook on it just to be safe. I did not want a relationship or anything that would warrant Valentine's gifts from Hunter. Ever. I didn't want a relationship with anyone in this town.

And what I'd told Wolf about my first time had definitely been a lie. That had not been sex that would rock my or any-one else's world—it had just been an experiment. A test run gone wrong. Did it count as sex when you didn't even feel it? I hadn't yet found a good candidate for a *real* first time, so I guess I still considered myself 80 percent virgin.

I was just a few miles from home when my cell beeped with a text. Glancing at it—the roads were barren, and I was driving slowly enough that a quick glance at the cell was safe-ish—I wondered if maybe Sadie had forgotten her cardigan in my car or something.

Fudge.

It was friggin' Hunter, inquiring about my whereabouts. I hit delete and focused on the road ahead. With my parents' holiday party on the horizon for next weekend, Hunter had redoubled his efforts, clearly confident that with the right level of attention and irritation, I would give it up to him again this year at the party.

That. Wouldn't. Happen.

(Probably.)

**3.** **THE REASON I WAS STILL 80 PERCENT**
virgin and 100 percent unattached would be easily understood
if you spent sixth period with Vic Burrows. Vic is my biology
lab partner, and our fifty minutes together every afternoon help
to underscore my frustration with our small-town existence.
He is the stud of our school—his hotness is in part due to
the fact that he drives a four-wheeler or snowmobile to school
every day. That doesn't really do it for me, and I am something
of a freak because of it.

"You are ... butt ugly ... to meeee." Vic sang this quietly, to the tune of "You Are So Beautiful." He'd composed this song sophomore year, and it seemed he still found it an awesome vocal masterpiece. It wasn't a ballad he'd devised specially for me, but as his lab partner I was the sixth-period object of Vic's affection, and at this moment he was serenading me with his tune as we dissected the leg muscles of a formaldehyde-soaked fetal pig. "Come on, Chaz, sing along."

"Your voice is so luscious; I wouldn't want to interfere," I deadpanned. "Please, carry on."

He grinned, revealing a chipped front tooth—user error when he'd tried to open a can of MGD with his mouth. "You haven't been cruising lately," he said, slicing his knife through a tendon that caused the pig's leg to flip up against my hand. "I've been watching for you."

"Astute observation," I replied. Cruising is our town's favorite pastime: Everyone drives their truck up and down Milton's short main drag, gaping at the people driving past them going the other way. At the end of town you whip a U-turn in the gas station lot and go back the other way. In the summer people walk up and down the strip a little bit, and then it makes sense—but when they drive up and down the street just for the hell of it, it's really, really weird.

I was into cruising for a while, back in ninth and tenth grade, when I still thought there were guys with potential in our town. But now that I was a senior, I knew my options, and they weren't pretty. I was confident that the love of my life—if that kind of thing even existed—did not live here, and thus cruising lost its appeal. "Cruising is bad for our carbon footprint," I said solemnly.

"You don't have to walk—don't worry about your feet," Vic chuckled. "You could ride in my truck."

"Oh!" I said lamely. "That'd be super fun!"

Vic looked honestly surprised. "Nice. Come out with us tonight."

"Oh, shoot." I snapped my fingers and pouted a little. "I have to work tonight—shift at Matt's. Another night, I guess."

"That's cool. Maybe we'll stop by and get some fries or something? Will you hook us up?" He winked, and I couldn't help but smile. He was charming, if you were into a Vic kind of guy. I wasn't, but as a chick I could see the allure that made him appealing for the rest of the girls in my class.

The bell rang then, and I called out, "I *might* hook you up, Vic—see you tonight, maybe?"

Vic and I have a good game going. Neither of us is into the other, but it's nonetheless fun to flirt just a little bit. I've known for a while that I don't fit into my town, but I try to make the most of my time here in Milton. If I had a crap attitude about it, I certainly would be one bitter chica. Bitter and mopey I am not—but that doesn't mean I'm not ready to hit the County Road and get out of Milton as fast as possible after graduation. To where, I know not.

"I got my letter, Chaz!" Sadie was suddenly next to me, breezing up with a trail of sweet strawberry scent behind her. "I got my letter from Macalester!"

"And?" I watched Sadie's face and already knew.

"I got in, Chaz!"

I hugged her immediately. Sadie had applied early decision at Macalester, one of Minnesota's super-cool and super-expensive private colleges. It had been her first choice forever, and she'd been freaking about getting her acceptance letter for the last three weeks. Her future had been planned for years—she even had a little teddy bear wearing a Macalester sweatshirt; she'd named it Mac and still slept with it every night. How cute (yuck) is that?

"When did you go home to check your mail? God, I'm so proud of you!" I hugged her again.

Sades blushed. "I've had my dad on high alert—he promised to bring it right away if it came. He pulled me out of calc last period, which was pretty sweet. Chaz, this means we'll be so close to each other next year! We can have dorm sleepovers and stuff!"

I cringed. Partly because I dreaded the notion of a dorm

sleepover, but primarily because I hadn't yet applied to any schools. I was *just* about to miss the mid-December priority deadline for applying to the U of M in Minneapolis, but I was keeping that little piece of information to myself. As far as my parents and Sadie were concerned, my application had been completed and shipped off right after Thanksgiving, and I was just waiting for the admissions website to refresh with a big, black "WELCOME" across the top.

In truth I still wasn't sure I'd be ready for college next year. I had no clue what I wanted to do with my life, and I wasn't so keen on shelling out thousands to sit around and play beer pong with a bunch of people in a dorm. I knew I'd be stuck in a work-study program to pay my way anyway, so a little part of me wondered if maybe I should hold off on college for a year, save up some cash, check out another part of the country by doing AmeriCorps or something, and try to figure out what I wanted to do with my life. I wasn't even sure a year would give me the answers I need, but at least it would be a start.

See, the future freaked me out, and I didn't have any easy answers about what I was going to do with my life. It seemed like everyone else did, and that scared the hell out of me. Sadie and I had never discussed it, and everyone just assumed I'd go on to great things, then return to Milton to pay it forward, I guess. What the hell was wrong with me that that sounded like a living hell? Why did I feel like I was committing a sin by not having a solid plan for myself?

"Yeah, dorm sleepovers." I slammed my locker and grinned at Sadie. "I probably won't find out about the U until May, though, so let's not buy the sleepover snacks just yet, okay?"

Sadie rolled her eyes. "Chaz, you're number one in our class—I don't think you have to worry about getting into the U, you goof!" Sadie is so *good*. Who uses the word "goof" in real conversation? People who sleep with bears that wear college sweatshirts before they're even *in* college, that's who.

"Well, we'll see," I said, heading off in the direction of last-period gym. I didn't want to talk about college. "I just want to get through this week and enjoy two weeks of blessedly school-free winter break. Then we can talk about college, okay?"

"Beep! Beep!" Sadie was waving her arm in the air. "Warning!" she cried. "Emotional constipation warning!"

I laughed. "Seriously, Sade, chill." I had jokingly told Sadie a while ago that she could warn me when I was closing myself off à la my mom. I had dubbed my mom's lack of openness "emotional constipation"—you can never get anything that resembles honest feelings out of her, and it pisses the hell out of me. "I'm not being emotionally constipated. It's not like I'm keeping something from you."

LIE! I yelled at myself inwardly. I was keeping a lot from Sadie, and she was the only person I even trusted. I don't want to be private and secretive, but when it comes to talking about *me*, I start to get a little freaky. I can easily talk about sex or other people's feelings or share my advice on just about any topic (granted, my recommendation is usually the opposite of what one should actually do). But talking about me, the deep-down, secret, private me . . . that's a skill I'm still working on.

I can be honest with *myself* to a fault, but there's a thin plastic shield melded to my body that keeps people out of my emotional private parts. And discussing college or the future or anything that involved a discussion of my life—the real life that would start post-Milton—was the equivalent of discussing my coochie, if I were to continue with that metaphor. I wanted to get out of town as soon as possible, and I knew it was stupid that I didn't yet have a perfect plan in place for how that could happen. It was eating me up.

"Let's celebrate after school, okay?" I suggested, eager to steer conversation away from the application process, et cetera. "Come over? I can give you a lift home on my way to work."

"I'm going to Trav's after school." Sadie smiled. "Can we hang out later this week?"

"For sure. Go celebrate with Trav, you little slut," I purred. She knew I was kidding. Sadie is so not a slut—she's in loooooove, and sex for her is sacred. She and Trav have been together for two years, and it was, like, a massive milestone when they finally did the deed.

The bell rang, and Sadie practically floated down the hall toward class.

I lingered by my locker for a few more minutes, then high-tailed it to class—I had a 4.0 GPA to maintain, and tardiness was a shit reason to risk a grade. Even if I wasn't going to college.

When Sexy Sebastian showed up at Matt's that night, I wasn't surprised. But I did hide under the bar, for just a few seconds, to check myself over. It's not that I gave a rat's ass what I looked like (yeah, that is a lie), but I for sure needed a sec to make certain I didn't have damp pits. Because pit stain isn't hot, and hot was what I was going for.

Angela had called me out on that instantly when I'd shown up for work that night. "Tight jeans, huh?" She gave me a little wink. She wasn't subtle, so it's not like I needed to read between the lines. I knew she'd carry on. "Hoping the cute boy from table six will show again?"

"No." I lifted my eyebrows at her.

"Liar."

I didn't need to get into this with Angela, so I walked away.

ERIN DOWNING

I usually tried to work only one shift during the school week, but this week was a little crazy at Matt's because of the holidays and all. So I'd agreed to take a few extra shifts, and now that Sebastian was in the picture and seemed to like the taste of our meat, I was glad I had. I could only hope they didn't have food at his dad's house and he'd be eating with me every night.

"Hey." I strolled over to his table when he showed up. The girl hormones that suddenly controlled my every move were making my stomach clench and my palms sweaty. I blinked more than usual. I didn't like my body to mess with me like this—I preferred to make the decision about when to freak, and I definitely didn't want to be freaking right now.

He looked up slowly, deliberately toying with me. "Hi." His smile was teasing me with that same subtle sexuality that made me want to scream. Did he feel it too?

"Back for more, huh?"

His grin widened. "My dad's not used to feeding two, and he seems to think I'm still a kid. The choices were mac and cheese or SpaghettiOs. I chose to go out instead."

"You're spending your two weeks of dad custody going out to restaurants alone? Doesn't that defeat the purpose of court-mandated quality time?"

"He works until nine every night. We hang out in the

morning before he takes off." Sebastian laid his menu on the table and looked up at me.

"Right." I pulled my order pad out of my back pocket and held a pen at the ready. I didn't want to seem like some sort of leech, even though what I really wanted was for him to invite me to sit down again. Good God, that makes me sound like a girl.

"Any specials tonight?"

That was the end of the chitchat. I took his order and dropped it off for Wolf; then things got busy, and I couldn't linger around his table, even though I wanted to. Just as I was delivering Sebastian's order—a grilled cheese and fries with a side of wilted lettuce with oil (aka house salad)—to his table, Vic and his buddies bounded through the front door.

"Hey, Chaz." Vic pulled off his snowmobiling face mask and brushed the snow off his big, thick jacket. "We came to collect."

I stole one last look at Sebastian, then walked away to greet Vic and his crew. "That sounds like a mob threat, Vic. You don't do mob well—your Minnesota accent is an eensy bit thick." Vic, Casper, and Jacob settled into one of the tables in Angela's section, but I waved at her to let her know I'd cover. It would be completely unfair for me to make her have to deal with them— Vic was sort of a problem I'd created and invited in.

"Sexy jeans," Vic assessed loudly. "Your ass looks good in those." His hand reached out to give me a little pat on the tush, but I wrapped my fingers around his wrist and twisted with all my might. I didn't want him to be confused about where I drew the line. He cringed, then shot me an apologetic smile. He isn't a total barbarian—you just have to know how to deal with him.

Tina Zander, who Vic had dated/toyed with off and on since eighth grade, had walked in moments before, and she watched the hand-approaching-my-ass move carefully. She shot me one of her icky looks, and I smiled sweetly back at her. It's not as if I was trying to get it on with her man. I didn't want there to be any confusion about that—frankly, I was more concerned about Tina getting the wrong impression than I was about Vic himself. He was mildly intelligent, but Tina had psycho-girl emotions acting as her puppet master, so who knew when she'd go all crazy on me and assume Vic and I were undercover lovers? "Hey, Tina," I said. "Want a Coke or something?"

"Vic," she whined, sliding into the booth next to him. "I'm thirsty."

"Right," I muttered under my breath. "I'll get you guys a pitcher," I said more loudly. "Diet, right? On me."

I don't like to give out freebies—they come out of my

tips—but I felt like I had to show Tina she didn't need to freak about me. In a town this small a less-than-ordinary girl does not need enemies. And Less-Than-Ordinary could be my screen name. (Of course it isn't. I'm not that keen on waving a giant freak flag. Come on.)

While I filled Tina's pitcher, I glanced over at Sebastian. He had finished eating and was staring out the window, watching snow flutter down on Vic's snowmobile parked on the front sidewalk. He looked so totally out of place, with his styled hair and the slightly-too-tight cut of his jeans. Vic he wasn't. When I peeked at him again, I saw him pull a twenty out of his wallet and set it on the table.

Then he stood up, looked over at me, and winked. I set the pitcher of Coke on the bar and cut him off at the door before he could get his coat on. "You need change," I announced.

"I'll be back tomorrow," he said. "Or the next day. You can owe me."

We were in the corner of the restaurant, right next to the door. It was dark, and the noise of the bar was a little more muted there. I knew he could hear me when I murmured, "I'd be happy to pay you back." I'm not sure what came over me—those pesky sex genes again, apparently—but I needed him to know what I was thinking. It wasn't until I'd said it that I realized I sounded like some sort of hooker, but I hoped he realized that wasn't what I meant. For him I'd do sex for free. For no one would I do sex for money—*ick*.

Sebastian didn't respond, but he leaned toward me as he maneuvered his arm into the sleeve of his coat. It meant nothing, but I felt my breath catch as his face passed within a few inches of mine. I longed to reach out and let my lips grab his to suck him up against me. He smelled like cinnamon gum and French fries and sauna soap. It seemed like he could sense my body tensing up as he got close to me—I noticed him pause as he zipped his coat; then he looked at me in that sexy, mysterious way once more.

"Good night, Chastity," he said; then he walked through the door and into the snowstorm. When I delivered the pitcher of Coke (*Drink up, Tina! Regular Coke!*) to my classmates, Vic had Tina in his lap and was rubbing her ass. There was something about that scene that fired me up in a way you can't even imagine.

I wanted Sebastian.

I needed Sebastian.

And all I could think about as I watched Vic's hand crudely stroke Tina's thigh was the fact that I would have Sebastian. That sexy, unsuspecting boy from North Carolina had no idea what he was in for.

Neither did I.

**. "HEY, DAD." I TOSSED MY BAG OVER**
the back of the couch after school the next day and shuffled
into the kitchen, where my dad was making bread. My dad's
a part-time domestic. He works three-quarters time at the
bank as a teller, then comes home and preps dinner for Mom
and me.

Mom is a full-time socialite (yes, in a town of mere thousands. . . . It's more like social-lite) who seems to think we
can make ends meet through volunteer work and community
building. It's cool that she likes to help other people, but she

sometimes forgets that our little family unit could use a little of her TLC directed inward.

"How was school, pumpkin?" See what I mean about me not fitting in with my parents? They're total goody two-shoes.

"Fine," I muttered in the general direction of my dad, grabbing an apple from the fridge. "When will the bread be ready?"

"Half an hour—but it's for the party, so I'm popping it straight in the freezer."

Oh, shit. The holiday party. "Saturday, right?" I asked, knowing full well that my parents' party was always the first Saturday of school break. They wanted to host the first party of the official Christmas season, and they had unofficially claimed the day as theirs for the past five years.

My dad nodded, punching the dough under his fat fist. He was sweating, and suddenly he looked older to me. And fatter. When had he become old and fat? It freaked me out a little, and I wanted to hightail it out of there. "Well, it's been real," I said, slinking out of the kitchen and up the stairs to my room. "Call me when the bread's done." As if he could keep me away from fresh-baked bread—freezer, my ass.

"Chastity?" I looked at him over the banister. He was peering out of the kitchen, his sweatshirt all covered in flour. There was a little in his beard, too. "You got a hug for your old dad?"

How's a girl supposed to resist that? As lame and emotionally stunted as my mother is, my dad's a real gem in the sweetness department. He's not exactly always there for me—let's just say, we have our differences . . . of opinion, of attitude, of dreams in life. But when it comes to trying to make me feel loved, my dad wins the blue ribbon. I sighed hugely (don't want to give it up too easily) and tromped back down the stairs. I rolled my eyes, then gave my big dad a tiny squeeze. He felt so soft and squishy—just like his bread dough—and I wished I could have turned out to be the kid they should have had.

But wishes don't always come true, which is why he and I are family. We make it work and stumble our way through. Someday, maybe, we'll all have a nice, hearty chuckle about how I was switched at birth and my real family is a pack of nomads who conceived me at an outdoor concert and live off the land. But for now I continue to play the part of my parents' strange daughter—while they wait for the angel that is their real little girl to be returned by an overly smiley talk show host who will drag me away while they all live happily ever after in the life that should have been.

I pulled away from my dad and ascended to my room. I tugged my jeans off and dug through my closet for my fleece-lined running pants. It wasn't snowing, it was above the official "freezing" mark, and I didn't have to work that night, which meant I could squeeze in a run before dark.

By high school definitions I'm a runner. In a town as small as Milton you either are a joiner or you aren't. But if you choose to exclude yourself from extracurricular activities, you are labeled a freak and suspected of planning a terrorist plot against the joiners. There are only two nonjoiners in my class, and they mostly just sit home and play video games all day. Alone. That seems really lame.

As previously mentioned, I have no interest in self-selecting myself into a life of loneliness and pain, so I joined the cross-country team back in seventh grade. As I see it, running is the sport that takes the least amount of coordination, doesn't involve any complicated cheers, and is nice and portable. I like that. Even though the season ended over a month ago, I am pretty well hooked and try to get out for a little heart-pumping action whenever I can.

My usual running route takes me down the long, unpopulated road that leads to my house and my house alone (we are located on a plot of land that can definitely be defined as "rural"). After a mile or so I turn onto the main road—also known as "the only road out of Milton"—past the middle/high school, and I circle around Sadie's house before heading back home. It definitely gets stale to always jog the same route, but there aren't a lot of options for variety when your town only has one main thoroughfare.

That day, however, I decided to shake things up and jog slightly beyond my usual U-turn spot to go by the house I knew to be Sebastian's dad's place. It was a tiny little house, slightly smaller than Matt's Bar, and suffered from a serious case of neglect. I hadn't ever really paid much attention to it before, but now that Sebastian and I had shared fries, I felt at liberty to take a peek around. At best Sebastian would be hanging around the front of the house and would invite me in for fun and games. At worst I'd get a few extra minutes in my run.

I slowed my pace, then actually converted to a walk to boost the odds that he might see me. I realized I was being a huge stalker, but given that he was only in town for a few weeks over Christmas break, I had to take the bull by the horns and go after what I wanted. That didn't mean I was going to walk up to his door in my sweaty state, but if I slowly meandered past and he just happened to see me from the big front window, I wouldn't be crushed.

Due to the fact that my life isn't a made-for-TV movie, no one was anywhere to be seen at Sebastian's place. All I noticed as I sashayed past his house was a reflection of myself in the window, looking kinda cute with two ponytails swinging out from under my lightweight hat. I picked up the pace, quickly bringing my speed up to a run to hustle toward home. The sun went down long before five, and I had two miles left to get back.

I had just kicked my speed up to do an interval as I shot past Matt's, when I spotted Sebastian walking down Main Street, wearing the most adorable little winter hat and that alluringly puffy jacket. He saw me before I noticed him, and he was obviously watching me coming closer. I slowed to a walk again, my heart racing from both the burst of speed and the anticipation of being close to him again. Maybe I *was* in a TV movie. . . . This was a little surreal and a classic case of romantic coincidence. If you believed in that brand of nonsense.

"A runner." He stated the obvious.

"Yep. Where're you off to? Another meal at Matt's?"

He grinned, holding up a thin plastic bag with a gallon of milk and a stick of butter inside. "Are you working tonight?" I shook my head, and he said, "Then I guess not."

It was the answer I wanted to hear. Some little indication that he had, in fact, been coming into Matt's at least partly to see me. "Mac and cheese tonight? Will you survive on your own?"

He cocked his head, still grinning at me with that amused

smile that made me want him and fear him all at once. "I think I'll make it. Will you?"

I loved him.

I hated him.

He *so* knew he had me. I said nothing. We just looked at each other, his eyes searching mine.

"I'd better get home, Chastity." He looked at the ground—his confidence seemed to break for a split second. But just moments later he looked up again, collected and calm and distant. "Later." He took off down the block. I stared after him until he turned at the corner, on his way back to his dad's house.

I was home in fifteen minutes flat, so distracted by my obsession with this stranger that I ignored the burning in my lungs and the knots in my thighs. Why couldn't I have had a hot boy to mind-fuck during the season? Maybe I would have actually placed in a meet. The only times I'd won anything since joining cross-country were races we ran against our own teammates in time trials, when Brianna Jenson and Kimber Mathias were sick. I wasn't the star of the team, but that made me blend in nicely, so I could simply hide from scrutiny and excessive praise.

After a hot shower I locked the door to my room and wandered around naked for a while. I'm no nudist, so don't think I get off on this sort of thing, but a website I found once suggested that spending some time with yourself naked will give you greater confidence when naked in the presence of a lover. Heh heh.

The word "lover" cracks me up, but that advice seems sound. I don't really mind my body, but the idea of getting nudie with someone and just putting it all out there for critique and comment is a little daunting.

My cell rang—it was buried inside the covers on my bed, so I lay down and answered. "Hey, Chaz." Hunter's voice barreled through the phone.

"What can I do for you, Hunter?" I asked, imagining what Hunter would say if he knew I was in my birthday suit, lying in bed. I could imagine how his breath would come in those short, eager bursts that I recalled from our afternoon together last year. The thought of how much he'd want to put himself inside me—coupled with the reminder of how hot Sebastian had looked in the late afternoon sunset—made my skin tingle. I let my hand slip down my body, touching myself the way I wanted Sebastian to.

"I just wanted to say hey." Hunter's voice broke into my sexual fantasy, an intruder in my dreams. Distracted, I let his voice slink into the scene in my mind, my thoughts wandering to how he had pushed against me last year. Maybe it was worth trying with him again this year?

"Hey," I said quietly back. "Are you coming to my parents' party next weekend?" My breath caught a little as my fingers found a sensitive spot.

Hunter cleared his throat. I imagined his cheeks were flushed, the embarrassment of last year flooding over him. "Do you want me to come?" He tried to sound seductive, but it came out too eagerly, too full of desire to give him any control of the situation. He was clearly putty in my hands, waiting for the okay from me to come over and try to show that he could be a worthwhile sex toy.

"Yes."

"Yes?" Hunter sputtered, his voice cracking.

"Yeah," I said again. "I want you to come to the party."

He paused. I could tell he wanted to ask if I was inviting him to come just for the party, or if that implied that this year's party would end the way last year's had. Finally, he managed to say, "This Saturday, right?"

"Mm-hmm," I moaned, my fingers turning circles on my body.

"Are you okay, Chaz?"

"I'll see you Saturday, Hunter. Don't forget to bring a condom." Then I hung up and let the fantasy that brought Sebastian into my room wash over me.

*　　*　　*

When my mom knocked at my door nearly an hour later, I was sound asleep. I stretched like a cat, ignoring her chirping voice. Eventually, the sound of the chirping turned to something more like yelping, and I rolled out of bed. I threw my sweats on and pulled a dirty Matt's T-shirt on over my braless body. I twisted the lock on my knob and opened the door to face my mom. "Yes?"

"I've been calling you for twenty minutes." She gave me the once-over, as if trying to figure out if I had some secret hidden lover in my lair who was now tucked slyly under a corner of my bed, hiding. *I wish.* "It's time for dinner. Your dad made meat loaf."

I followed her dutifully down the stairs and plunked down at the kitchen counter. My mom looked at me again, one eyebrow curved up into a peak. She needn't have said anything, since that peaked eyebrow is always accompanied by nagging. That day's nagging sounded like this: "Do you ever wear those khaki slacks I bought you before school started?"

"I told you, I don't like khakis." This response, courtesy of *moi*, was delivered in the tone that is adored by mothers the world over.

"Don't take that tone with me." The scold, followed by the weak compliment: "You look so nice when you put a little care into your appearance."

"I think I look nice now." I needn't continue with the details—the conversation progressed for another ten minutes or so, at which point I finished my meat loaf and stood up to return to my room. Meanwhile my dad just sat there silently, wishing that talk show host would show up now and switch me with their real kid.

I could only hope the switch would happen before the holiday party. Because I had no idea how it would all go down, and I had promised Hunter a little bit of nookie I wasn't sure I wanted to deliver.

**5.**   **"HUMP."**

"Screw."

"Shag."

"Making love."

"Carpet munching."

"Ewww! Chaz! Don't be vulgar."

"What?" I laughed. "Fine, bonking. But I'm up two."

Sadie furrowed her precious brow, trying so hard to one-up me in our tasteful game of synonyms. "Making whoopee!" she squealed. "Getting laid!"

"Flick her wick."

"No." Sadie crossed her arms. "You just made that up. Go again."

"Mating."

"Intercourse."

"Hot beef injection," I beamed. "Horizontal hula. Mattress dancing. I could go on all day."

Sadie stuffed her face into my bed pillow, hiding. Her muffled voice muttered, "Chaz, there's something seriously wrong with you." She looked up at me and grinned.

"I am very cute."

"Agreed. But in that grody, sick sort of way."

"At least it's not sick the way you've been sick for the last two weeks." I watched as Sadie rolled over so she was looking up at the ceiling. She looked thinner than usual—her squeezable, chubby cherub cheeks were more angular—and there was still sort of a sick pallor to her skin. "Are you gonna heave on my bed?"

She pulled a magazine off my bedside table and began to rip pages out of it. "I don't think so. The worst seems pretty much over."

I lay next to her and watched what she was pulling out of the magazine—I suspected she was on the hunt for a new hairstyle. "I'm glad. You look a little . . . um, dead."

Sadie lifted an eyebrow. "Um, thanks?"

"Just eat up to get your girlish glow back, okay?" I kissed her cheek. "Now, getting back to the subject," I said, eager to continue the conversation that had led into our sexual synonyms throw-down. "How's the sex?"

"It's not about sex," Sadie said, looking all dreamy. "I am completely in love."

"That's pretty obvious." Sadie's happiness was infectious, and nothing made me happier than seeing my best friend feeling the way she does about Trav. Trav is kind of a dip, if you ask me, but he treats Sadie like a princess, and she deserves someone like that. So even though he isn't exactly *my* type, I don't need to fake the enthusiasm. "But the sex . . ."

"Yes!" Sadie threw the magazine down and covered her face with her hands, knowing what I was asking. "It's better." The first few times Sade and Trav did it, Sadie had pretended things were awesome and romantic and perfect, but I finally got her to admit that she was woefully uncomfortable the whole time, and went home less than impressed. I had armed her with what appeared to be quality literature I'd found online, and had suggested she study for sex with the same passion she used to study for American history exams.

"Does it rock your world?"

"You need to get laid." Sadie rolled onto her side to face

me. "I want you to get out of my business and get into some of your own."

"I do too." My mind flashed to the fantasy of Sebastian, then wandered off to the reality of Hunter. After a long pause I finally said, "I'm thinking about trying again with Hunter."

Sadie sat up and leaned against the wall, her eyes wide with surprise. "You wouldn't!"

"I would," I admitted. "There aren't any more tasty options, so I better take what I can get."

"What about Sebastian?"

I shook my head—he clearly wasn't going to be easy to figure out—and said, "What's the chance that's going to happen, really? Gotta settle for the best Milton has to offer."

"What's wrong with waiting?" Sadie and I have different ideas about sex. She had always intended to wait until marriage—but modified her promise when confronted with love—and I wanted a sufficient level of sexual experience before I settled down. *If* I ever settled down. I can't explain how my attitude toward sex was formed, but I've just never had the same monumental fear and anticipation of losing it that many other girls in my town do. Sex exists for a reason, and it wouldn't be offered up as an extracurricular activity if it were something we weren't supposed to do.

"I'd rather not."

"At least your mom will be happy." Sadie shrugged. "She loves Hunter."

"I'm not doing this to make my mom happy. Besides, it's not like we'll be entering into a relationship or holy matrimony or anything. It's just sex."

Sadie frowned. "It's not *just* sex, Chaz."

"We have to agree to disagree. Again." The truth was, I was scared of the sex that *wasn't* just sex. I didn't want sex plus. I wanted to experience the physical piece of it, which was why Hunter was a rather superb choice. I knew there wasn't much risk of me developing anything beyond the experimentation stage with Hunter. The emotional bullshit Sadie was always talking about scared the hell out of me. *Blech*.

"Fine." Sadie resumed her magazine reading. "But maybe you *should* consider a relationship with Hunter. He's really sweet."

"That's completely settling, Sade. I don't want sweet. I want sinful." I grinned and pulled out last year's yearbook, flipping to Hunter's picture. I pointed to his puffy hair and dopey, close-mouthed grin. "I want sexy. I want sizzle."

Sadie laughed. "You're not going to get sizzle with Hunter. I can guarantee that."

"So you do get it!" I slammed the yearbook closed. "You know I'm not looking for someone who's going to analyze my feelings and comfort me when I've had a shit day—that's what you're here for." My best friend rolled her eyes, tearing a picture of Katie Holmes's latest haircut out of the magazine, then holding it next to her face. I shook my head no and continued. "What you and Trav have is great, but there isn't a Trav for me here in Milton. I don't want a Trav here—I want to get the hell out and look for my guy somewhere else. Emotionless fucking suits me just fine for now. Or it would if I could even get that."

"I know you want to get out of Milton, Chaz. But don't do anything stupid."

I stared at her in disbelief. "This from the girl who's sneaking around, having sex in her boyfriend's car? Is that what I'm supposed to aspire to?"

"We did it in his room a few weeks ago when his parents were gone," Sadie giggled. "He lit candles and everything. It was really sweet."

"If I lit candles with Hunter, I bet his hair would catch fire."

"Fair enough," Sadie agreed. "But just be careful with Hunter. I'm not entirely sure you and he have the same sensibility about these sorts of things. You said it yourself—he's the best thing this town has to offer, and what you're planning may be more fucking *with* him than fucking him. That's all I'm saying."

She was totally wrong. Right?

The roar of a snowmobile echoed off the brick school wall on Thursday afternoon, the second-to-last day before winter break. There was a biting chill in the air, and most people were hustling to the buses or their cars. Me? I had forgotten my hat in the car when my dad had dropped me off that morning, and now I was bracing myself for the frozen walk to Matt's. Matt had begged me to start my shift right after school that day, since business was really picking up as people came home for the holidays, zipping in from their shiny new towns to visit those of us still stuck in Milton.

This time of year was always like a big, happy town reunion. The shops on our main drag did half their business in the few days leading up to Christmas, and everyone spent evenings gathering at Matt's with old friends and family. The visitors who didn't know any better went to Gina's or Café Cheapo, but the Milton originals knew Matt's was the place to be. The holidays couldn't fool me, however. All I wanted for Christmas was a ticket out of here.

I took a deep breath and stepped out the front door of school into the wind. I had only taken a few steps when the roar of the snowmobile growled behind me and whirred to a stop. "You need a ride, pretty lady?" Vic grinned at me from beneath his full-face-mask hat (yes, the kind with two eye holes and a circle for the mouth). He revved the motor and patted the seat behind him. I considered my options and promptly hopped aboard. "Where to? My place?" Vic grinned.

"Matt's, please," I replied. "Though your offer is certainly tempting."

Vic looked back at me with eyes wide inside their knit holes. "Really?"

"Not really." I narrowed my eyes at him before wrapping my arms around his midsection and hiding my face in his back. "Freezing here . . . can we get a move on?"

"Right." The snowmobile roared to life, and we were at Matt's in less than a minute. Vic rolled the bottom of his face mask up to blow me a kiss. Then he slapped my ass . . . again.

"Why?" I asked, backing away from his snowmobile. "What would Tina say if she saw that? Are you trying to get me scratched to death?"

Vic chuckled. "I guarantee Tina's already pissed at you, since I was supposed to give her a ride home from school— but I picked you up instead." He shrugged. "A little competition is healthy for chicks."

"Seeing as how I have no interest in any part of that competition, I'm going inside now. Thanks for the lift." I opened the front door to Matt's, and the very first person I saw was Hunter. He was sitting with his mom and my parents at a table in the middle of the restaurant, and all four of them were staring at me like I was topless.

Before I bothered saying anything, I turned to look back out the window to see how much of my Vic interaction they'd witnessed. And there in front of the window sat Sebastian. As usual he was busy watching the action on the street. He turned to look at me, and that slow, seductive smile passed across his face. Today was going to be a jolly good time, of that I was certain.

"Christmas comes early for Chaz," I muttered under my breath.

I could hear my mom asking Hunter, "Was that Vic Burrows?"

After a quick smile in Sebastian's direction, I reluctantly wandered over to my parents' table. "What's the occasion?" I smiled hugely at Miriam and my mom. My dad didn't even look up from his piss-water coffee. He looked like he'd been dragged along for the ride.

"Miriam and I just finished Celebrate Christmas rehearsal at church." Celebrate Christmas is the choral "event" that my mom lives life for. For our small-town church choir, Christmas Eve services are the equivalent of a performance at Carnegie Hall. "When we picked Hunter up at school, he reminded us you were working all afternoon." He did? I looked over at

Hunter, who was flushing a deep shade of magenta. "We just ordered burgers!" My mom giggled, as though this were the most novel concept the world had ever heard. She's always watching her weight, so I suppose bacon-fat-fried hamburgers were sort of giggle-worthy.

"Well, isn't that fun?" I continued to smile. "I sure wish I could sit with you and enjoy a cozy little holiday lunch, but I'm afraid I need to hop to it."

Miriam Johnson looked at my mom, then back at me, and with a pinched half smile asked, "Are you and Vic Burrows an 'item' now?" Yes, she made air quotes around the word "item."

Nosy, nosy Mrs. Johnson. But, um, ew. "No, Miriam. Thanks for asking, though!" I traipsed off to the back room with no further explanation, where I wrapped myself in an apron and hoped the waitress costume would make me invisible to my family and their wannabe son-in-law. I willed that the apron would have the exact opposite effect on my man at table six.

Angela sashayed up and bumped my bony hip with her own. "Hey, sweetie."

"Are you covering my parents' table?" I begged.

She grinned. "Yeah. What a sweet family get-together," she teased. Angela had her suspicions about my history with Hunter. We'd never actually discussed it, but the clues were pretty obvious to someone who spent as much time with me as

Ange did. She wasn't necessarily the most astute individual, but Angela had a special eye for sex clues and relationship drama.

"Yes, isn't it?" I grabbed an order pad off the back counter and stuffed a couple pens in my back pocket. "Has it been busy?"

"Nah, but we're staffed up. Guess who's back in town?" Angela shot me the sultry look usually reserved for her boy toy of the month. I raised my eyebrows and waited for the announcement. "Danny!"

"Danny Idol?"

Angela snorted. "Danny Idol" was the pet name I'd assigned to Danny Pratt, one of Milton's most illustrious alums. During his junior year Danny had left Milton for two weeks to participate in the Hollywood round as an *American Idol* hopeful. He'd been booted off the show before he got even fourteen seconds of airtime. His only real claim to fame was being featured in a montage of performances during group week. His group had choreographed a boy-band-meets-line-dance mash-up sort of thing, and the producers had aired it as an example of a totally ridiculous performance. But that mattered little when Danny came home to Milton— he was hailed as a hometown superstar (complete with a winter parade and everything) and had lived his last year and a half of high school as a veritable celebrity.

Danny graduated last year and is now the front man for a rock band called Suck This that plays the coffee shop circuit around Northern Minnesota. Despite the fact that I totally made fun of Danny behind closed doors after the whole *Idol* thing, even I couldn't deny the fact that Danny was a major sexpot. I'd always had a little physical crush on him. "What's he up to?" I asked Ange casually.

"Winter break dishwasher."

"Here?" I paused. "At Matt's?"

Angela winked. This was new—she had become a winker in the last few days, perhaps something she'd picked up from watching TV. I didn't quite get the meaning behind the winks, but she looked kinda cute doing it, so I understood why she was trying to make it a regular new affectation. "His gigs don't pay, and his parents wanted him home for the holidays. So he managed to beg a few weeks' work off Matt."

Excellent, I mused. "Will he be treating us to a special performance over the holidays? Is Matt's hosting a Suck This gig to celebrate the return of the hometown hero?"

"Ask the hero himself," Angela suggested. "He's working this weekend, so you guys can get all caught up." She winked again, then headed back out to the front room to drop off my parents' burgers.

I hustled past their table as Ange delivered food, hoping

Mom (and, less likely, Hunter) would be distracted enough by the fatty beef that she would fail to notice me passing by. Sebastian was still holding his menu in one hand, book in the other, and had clearly not yet ordered. It was an unspoken thing between Angela and me that Sebastian was mine. She didn't approach him, and in exchange I'm sure she expected that I would give her all the gritty details if anything happened between us.

"Good afternoon," I purred, standing beside his table. "Aren't you a little early today?"

"Lucky me," he said dully. "I feel fortunate to have arrived early enough to see your charming boyfriend again." He smiled, and with it my insides wrapped into twisted spirals.

"He's not—"

"I know." Sebastian cut me off. "I've been paying attention."

"You have, have you?" *He has?* "And what have you learned?"

He glowed with pride. "Name Chastity, goes by Chaz. Runs cross-country. Single and flirty. Parents sitting fifteen feet away"—he motioned toward my parents with a subtle nod of his head—"with a boy who is clearly infatuated with their daughter."

So far, so observant. Overall I was unimpressed.

Then he continued in a lowered voice that forced me to put my hands on his table and lean in to hear him. "Wants a fast ticket out of her small town. Arms herself with an attitude that keeps people ten feet back."

I stared at him without saying anything. What did *he* know?

Against my will my eyes started to fill up with tears. *That* was his opinion of me? Clearly, I had made quite an impression. I swallowed against the hurt that burned my throat, and smiled. "You certainly are quick to judge." My hands remained on his table, holding myself up. He moved his hand across the table and put it near mine—but stopped short of actually touching me—while I willed myself to breathe again.

"It's not judging." He looked at me with an intensity that made me shiver, then pulled his hand away to pick up his menu.

"Okay. Do you want anything to eat, or are you just here to serve up an order of analysis and criticism?" I said this lightly, jokingly, in a voice that defied the rotten feeling in my stomach.

Sebastian looked down and pushed his book—*Nine Stories* by J. D. Salinger—across the tabletop. When he looked up again, his face was empty, the intensity from moments earlier gone and replaced by something vaguely amused and noticeably distant. "I shouldn't have said that. I'm sorry."

I wanted to say something that would bring the life back

to his face—as much as his comments had stung, there was something so blunt and understanding about them that I wondered what else he thought about me. The fact that he was analyzing me at all signified something. But it was clear from his expression that I'd dead-ended this avenue of conversation with my reaction, and we were back to the starting line— perfect strangers, waitress and customer, boy and girl. *Excellent work, Chaz.* "It's okay," I said finally.

"I'm going to wait to order, if that's okay with you." He opened his book to a dog-eared page.

"Take your time." As I walked numbly back toward the kitchen, my mom stopped me. She was obviously going to try to coordinate a nice, civil conversation between Hunter and me. Or worse, she was going to try to force me to sit with them, invite me to join them on the little family lunch happening at Matt's. "Chastity," she said, holding her napkin to her mouth to cover up any beef remnants that might be in her teeth. She nodded at me, then said, "You should tuck in your shirt. You look a mess." *Or that.*

I walked on. The afternoon was shaping up to be a real winner.

Things didn't get much better as the day went on. It was clear I'd completely eliminated any hope for anything beyond servitude with Sebastian—he didn't order anything more than a root beer and left before the dinner rush. Hunter—in a very uncharacteristic, Vic-like move—leered at me from his seat next to my dad and texted me to tell me I looked hot. He was clearly stung by my arrival on the back of Vic's snowmobile that afternoon, and it had whipped him into a competitive frenzy.

Hunter's efforts didn't help portray him as any sexier, but it didn't totally ruin his chances. At least he was making an effort to *try* to be more interesting. Truth be told I was looking forward to the holiday party that weekend. Because my only other options for action of any kind appeared to be as follows:

1) Hold out hope for a performance from Danny Idol
2) Order up a sample of Wolf's French fry
3) Issue a catfight throw-down versus Tina Zander for the highly desirable Vic Burrows
4) Pretend I had a chance in hell with Sexy Sebastian from North Carolina (who thought I was a closed-off bitch)

Looking at my menu of choices, it appeared that Hunter was easily the best option Milton had to offer.

**6.** **THE LAST DAY OF SCHOOL BEFORE**
winter break brought with it the joy and delight of Milton's
annual Snow Swing, the magic of which has always been lost
on me.

Snow Swing is my mom's dream come true—we'll leave
it at that.

So when I announced in late November that I had neither a date to the dance nor intentions to acquire one, my
mother almost canceled Christmas. However, she realized
that that, too, would have been of little import to me. Thus

she announced Christmas would stay, but we would find some other way to make me pay for my lack of reverence for Snow Swing. (Of course we both knew that the birth of Jesus was my mom's dream holiday and that canceling the festivities would have meant no holiday party. You see her dilemma.)

And so my punishment for the lack of Snow Swing enthusiasm was determined to be a complete surrender of power on my gown purchase—my mom had declared that I would be going to the dance whether I wanted to or not, and she had given herself buying power over my wardrobe for the night. I was to be a part of the "group" Sadie and Trav had cobbled together to make me feel like less of a dateless loser.

I *had* received an invite to the dance from dear Hunter, but I just wasn't willing to go there.

As soon as school let out the last day before break, Sadie grabbed me and the other girls in her group and we all piled into my car to go to my house to get ready together. Tegan and Jen—sweet girls who are on volleyball with Sadie—had bags filled with makeup that they'd brought to school that morning, and their moms were bringing their dresses to church choir that afternoon to give to my mom, who would bring them home with her. Sadie's mom worked at the bank with my dad, so the handoff of her goods was happening there. When we got to my house fifteen minutes after school let out, everything was organized and ready . . . except me.

I still hadn't seen the dress my mom had selected, I didn't know how to put on makeup without looking like a transvestite, and I was clearly the only girl in the group who had reservations about the Snow Swing. I guess somewhere deep down I was maybe a little excited about the dance—Punch! Dancing! Grand March!—but that deep-down me was struggling to surface.

While the other girls primped and primed and poufed in the bathroom, I sat on the toilet lid filing my nails and trying to polish them to a shimmery pink luster. But I kept getting glops of Tegan's polish on the bathroom sink, so Sadie had to take over for me. Sade could tell I was way out of my element, so after she was done with my nails, she pulled out some sort of magic potion and then a brush that she started fluffing around my face to make me look pretty.

Tegan studied herself in the mirror and wrinkled her nose. "I think I need more eyeliner."

Jen squeezed her eyelashes inside a contraption and handed what looked like a green colored pencil toward Tegan. "Sadie, you look great. Do you think tonight might be the night you and Trav will . . . ?" She broke off, giggling.

I got a look from my best friend that said, *don't say a word,* so I just sat there silently while the girls discussed Sadie's potential for sex with Trav (clearly, neither of them knew what I knew). Of course, not one of them ever actually used the word "sex," but we all knew what they were talking about.

Sadie blushed but finally admitted that she and Trav were definitely ready. "We've talked about it a lot, and I do, um, want to. But not tonight, since I'm doing a sleepover with you guys after—soon, though." She squeezed her eyes shut, smudging her mascara, embarrassed to be talking about this as "openly" as they were. Tegan and Jen both gasped. I rolled my eyes, confident that no one was looking at me.

"Are you on the pill?" Tegan asked, then looked like she wished she could take it back. "I mean, you don't have to tell me or anything."

Jen gaped at her friend's abruptness but then looked quickly to Sadie for the answer. "No, I'm not on the pill. But I definitely know I love him, so who knows what will happen?" Sadie admitted, busying herself with the brush—she'd been working on me for way, *way* too long, and I was getting impatient. I reached up to touch my face, and it felt like a thin sheet of paper had been laid across my cheek—it was smooth and sort of cold and remarkably hairless. "Foundation," Sadie muttered quietly, putting the brush down to switch over to eyeliner.

Jen and Tegan both bubbled on enthusiastically about how

much they wished they could be in love the way Sadie and Trav were. I was bored with the love talk and wished we could get into a more juicy conversation. When Sadie admitted that Trav had bought condoms, Jen twisted her purity ring nervously on her finger, as though talking about sex or touching or even thinking about sex were criminal. But to me it looked like she had about a million things to ask about what—exactly—Sadie and Trav had done together up to this point.

Tegan stuck out her lower lip in the mirror and pouted, "I don't even have a date to walk with me at Grand March, let alone someone who will kiss me at the end of the night."

"I'll walk with you during the Grand March. That way neither of us has to walk alone," I offered, knowing what the answer would be.

Tegan looked embarrassed when she said, "Oh, that's okay, Chaz. I don't want people to think we're, um . . ."

"Together?" I offered, eyebrows raised.

Sadie snorted, which made her hand slip and the eyeliner pencil shoot across my temple. She cleaned it up with a wet tissue and started fresh. As she worked her magic, she was popping Tums nonstop. Sade's stomach was still rumbly, so she was doing everything she could to make sure she wouldn't ralph on her dress or on Trav at the Snow Swing.

I will admit, when Sadie was done fixing me up, I looked

better. I wouldn't let her put the shiny stuff on my lips—that was where I drew the line. According to Tegan gooey lips were critical. According to me that was where the transvestite comparison came into the picture—and with boobs like mine I do need to worry about that sort of thing. It's my "boyish figure" that causes problems.

By the time my mom got home at five with Jen's and Tegan's dresses, we had resolved that Jen and Tegan were definitely both still virgins (though Tegan was anxious to move past first base) and Sadie was posing as one. No one asked me. We all had our makeup slathered on, and hair had been fluffed to perfection. Tegan and Jen looked like they'd been done up by the makeup girl at the Glamour Gals photo studio in the mall. I couldn't help but make some inner comparisons between girls going to a dance and hookers. Subtlety is apparently out this year.

Sadie looked pretty, as always. She had her hair twisted up in back, and her cheeks were rosy (she'd blushed them to compensate for the stomach ailment) and a little sparkly. She'd skipped the eye makeup, so she looked glamorous and natural. Sadie slipped her dress on and was absolutely stunning. She looked so grown-up and put-together and mature.

I, on the other hand, had just gotten my first glimpse of my dress for the ball, and I needed a fairy godmother to come and take it away. My mom had gone all out. It had bows (small ones, but they were there) and ruffles and was a putrid pink color. I didn't even know where she'd found something so hideous. It seemed impossible to me that a store would even carry something that garish. It was like an eighties movie gone wrong.

Jen and Tegan did their best to pretend it looked cute, but Sadie didn't even fake it. She just sort of gasped when I pulled the thing out of the bag and shook with laughter when I pulled it over my head. "I guess that's what you get for letting your mom pick your dress." She was in hysterics. "Maybe you should have pretended to care a little more, huh?"

"Heh, heh, heh," I said without laughing. "Come on, you guys. This is terrible. I can't go in this—would jeans cut it?" My mom had gone back downstairs, so I was alone with my friends.

All three of them looked at each other. Clearly, Jen and Tegan weren't comfortable enough with me to laugh about it. They didn't know me well enough to realize I didn't really take things like this too seriously. So they probably figured I was going to be all broken up about it and ruin their night by starting to cry and needing to stay home or something like that.

I wasn't going to pout about it, but this horror was just making me hate dances even more. It was also going to make it fully impossible for me to fly under the radar tonight. No one could miss me. I was a sight to be seen.

When we were all ready, the four of us paraded downstairs to where my parents were waiting in the living room. "Oh!" my mom gasped while my dad took pictures. "You girls look lovely."

"Really?" I muttered under my breath. "Nice pick, Mom."

Tegan, Jen, and Sadie were all glowing with pride and overzealous blusher application. We were already running late, so there was only time for a few pictures before we had to pile into the car. I was driving us to school, where we'd meet up with the guys before the Grand March. My parents were driving separately with the Johnsons, who were going to the Grand March despite the fact that Hunter wasn't going to the Snow Swing. He hadn't found a date, and he didn't want to go alone. *His* mom hadn't forced *him* to go. Lucky duck.

The Grand March has been around as long as Snow Swing itself has been a Milton tradition. It was also the main reason I wanted to skip out on the dance. Here's how Grand March works: Every parent, old person, underclassman, and curious neighbor all pile into our school auditorium seats, and all the seniors (and their dates where applicable) attending the dance parade across the stage before the festivities begin.

So when we got to school, the four of us headed to the

gym, which is where everyone was gathering for the march. "Will they notice if I just skip the Grand March?" I muttered to my friends as we walked through the hallways at school.

"Oh, Chaz, you can't!" Tegan said. "The Grand March is the most important part."

Sadie fixed me with a very firm look. "Just do it. You'll have fun."

"I have to walk across the stage alone when they announce my name." I felt sick. "Give me one of your Tums," I instructed Sadie. She just stared me down. How had I let my mother coerce me into doing this? I was walking the stage alone, no date. Though I guess that was better than being escorted by Hunter. "I look like a freak."

"You look pretty!" Tegan declared (lies!). "A lot of girls get announced alone—that way everyone in the audience will be focused on just us. We don't have to share the spotlight!"

Oh, if only that were my goal in life. To have the spotlight focused on only me. I really, really preferred to have other people make waves—I was just fine hanging back, thanks. Especially when it came to small-town crap conventions like the Snow Swing Grand March. I swallowed, suddenly somewhat ill. "Do I have time to go to the bathroom?"

Jen and Tegan both nodded yes, but Sadie shot me another look. This one said, *I know what you're up to,* and she grabbed my arm to pull me along to the gym, where most of our junior and senior classmates were gathered. It seemed highly unnatural to have the fancy dresses and suits lit up under the basketball hoops.

I glanced around, wondering how I was going to get through this night. I'm no drinker, but Vic's flask (I could see him taking a nip from it under the bleachers) looked mighty tempting right about then. Tina Zander saw me looking their way and lifted her leg up to wrap it around Vic's waist. She was wearing a strapless minidress—electric green.

"There's Trav," Sadie cried, grabbing my arm as Tegan and Jen hustled off to ooh over other people's dresses. "Doesn't he look so cute in his suit?" She beamed, watching Trav kicking awkwardly at the floor of the gym with a couple of his friends. Their dress shoes were leaving black streaks on the floor. When he spotted her, Trav's whole face lit up, and he came to greet her with a quick kiss.

"Oh, you two," I cooed. "Aren't you too cute?"

"You look great, Chaz," Travis offered generously, after lavishing praise on Sadie's adorable getup.

Sadie laid her head against his shoulder. I looked around for Tegan or Jen, desperate not to be the third wheel during Sadie and Trav's big night. Sadie must have sensed my discomfort, since she picked her head up and subtly slipped her hand into Trav's. Then she said, "We're really excited we could do this as a group. It will be so much more fun."

"Absolutely," I agreed, crinkling my forehead. "I'm sure you'll be thrilled I'm there when you're trying to make out later during a slow song." I sang, "Just the three of us, we can make it if we try . . . just the three of us."

Trav reddened. I don't think he knew that I knew as much as I knew. Basically, he probably had no clue she'd told me they were having sex. "We have plenty of time to be alone," Sadie said, then flushed. "I mean, tonight is about all of us hanging out together, right, Trav?"

"Yeah." He nodded, though I could tell he was hoping to end the night with a little nookie.

Our principal, Mrs. Jablonski, shouted out for attention then, calling, "Kids! Kids! Quiet up, please!" It cracked me up to hear her call us kids. Looking around the gym, it was clear everyone there thought they were far beyond kid stage. The hemlines were hiked, necklines were cut, and makeup had been poured on. We were anything but kids tonight.

And then, amidst the quiet of the gym, Vic let out a roaring, juicy burp.

Everyone laughed—ha ha, Vic!—and I realized why Mrs. Jablonski felt entitled to address us the way she did. "Listen up!" Jablonski called again. "We're ready to get started. I need girls to line up in alphabetical order. Boys, join your dates in their place in line. If you're alone, hang your head in shame and get ready for humiliation."

Yeah, she didn't say that last part. She actually told us loners to find our place in the alphabet, which meant I was fourth in line. Fourth. I had to march fourth; Bryan was fourth out of an entire junior and senior class. Curse a small town where a *B* name is that close to the front.

We lined up and started the parade toward the auditorium. Luckily, I was right behind Jen (Bruno) and Morris, so I had someone to chat with on the seemingly long walk down the hall. But as soon as we got to the side door to the stage, I was on my own again. I listened while Mrs. Jablonski welcomed the whole freaking town to the Grand March and recited some nonsense about the traditions of the Snow Swing. Then I heard applause, and the first pair of names were called.

Every time someone walked out on stage, the crowd went wild—different little pockets of people cheered for their neighbors and family members. When it was my turn, I walked out on stage with my head held high. My hands were hiding the bows on either side of my waist, which I hoped gave me a somewhat saucy, supermodel stance. I heard Angela yell "hot," but then the blood was pounding too hard in my ears to know if there were any other cheers.

I actually made it through the horror with no major snafus and took my place on the risers on the side of the stage to watch the rest of the lineup parade through. I couldn't see anything in the audience, since the lights were shining on us, melting makeup off faces. The rest of the march flew by, and before I knew it, they were calling Tina Zander and Vic Burrows to the front of the stage. The show ended when Tina turned her ass to the audience and Vic gave her five little slaps upside the rear end in front of the entire town. All the "kids" on stage laughed hilariously, while the audience bubbled with whispers and tsking.

We were hurried off the risers then and given our tickets to the dance as we hustled out the door of the auditorium. It's crap that they withhold tickets until after the Grand March. It forces people to participate in this totally freaked-up tradition, and I for one am not a supporter. It makes Milton feel even more miniscule and lame the way everyone in town feels so connected to high school traditions.

Sadie and Trav caught up to us as Jen, Morris, and I walked down the hall toward the cafeteria. Tegan cried out, "You guys! You guys!" and we all laughed and chattered on our way into the dance. I realized I was actually having fun, now that the Grand March was over. Without a date I got to dance to all the fast songs with the girls, and I hung out drinking punch and looking at everyone's outfits during the slow songs.

The only way the night could have been better was if Sebastian could have been there with me, holding me during the slow songs and sneaking off into the corner—where they kept the folded-up tables—to make out during some of the fast ones. If he'd seen my dress, he would have had no choice but to rip it off me—that's how heinous the thing was. No matter how little he liked me like that, the dress would have inspired him to get me naked.

"Do you wish Hunter were here?" Tegan yelled into my ear during one of the too-loud slow songs.

I looked at her like she was insane. "Hunter Johnson?"

"Yeah." Tegan smiled earnestly. "Aren't you guys, like, hanging out?" She noticed my expression then and said, "Sadie said you guys were maybe going to come to the dance together?"

"No."

"He's not bad," Tegan said, her teeth glowing vibrant white in the blue light that had just been turned on.

I considered that. "Not bad, huh? That's what I'm looking for."

"You make me laugh, Chaz." Tegan said this without laughing. "I mean, we don't have that many guys to pick from in Milton, right? Hunter isn't as gross as, like, Herbie Landon." She nodded her head in the direction of Herbie, who had come to the dance with Mary Appleton. They had been first in the Grand March lineup.

"Hunter's nice and all," I agreed, "but I'm definitely not dating him." Tegan was waiting for more, so I continued. "I guess I would rather be single than settle for someone who can be described as 'not as gross as Herbie Landon.'"

Tegan laughed out loud when I said that. "Yeah, I guess." But I could tell she didn't get it. She didn't get that I would rather be alone and not "in a relationship" than settle for someone who was "not as gross" as someone really, really gross. I was holding out hope for something real, someone who could rock my world. Something I couldn't find in Milton. Something I hoped I could find somewhere.

Sadie came over then and pulled us both back out onto the dance floor for a girls-only slow dance where we all hugged in a circle and laughed through the whole song. Before I knew it, the night was over, and we were all piling back into my car to drive back to my house for a sleepover.

When I pulled out my cell as we were getting into the car, I noticed I had a text. It was from Hunter and said: *You looked beautiful at the Grand March tonight.*

He had been there, sitting in the audience?

Oh, boy. The guy was whipped. Things were getting complicated.

**7.** **MY RELATIONSHIP WITH HUNTER**

was what we Minnesotans would call "different." When something is described as "different" here, it isn't necessarily good, and it isn't bad . . . but it *is* unconventional, and that is undoubtedly off-putting.

The situation with Hunter was thus: We had seen each other partially naked, we had swapped spit, and I knew exactly how his face contorted during an orgasm. Yet I barely knew him.

His favorite color?

His greatest fear?

His relationship with his parents?

I could only guess the answer to any of those things (though if my mom had that fake, pinched smile Miriam Johnson does, I would run screaming). There were pros and cons to my decision to let Hunter back into my room during this year's holiday party.

Pros: He was the best thing Milton had to offer and had an ample boy bit. He also didn't smell funny (some people do, and it definitely ruins a moment), *and* he'd kept our first attempt at sexual relations to himself. And he had been somewhat less wussy and pitiful as of late, which was somewhat appealing.

Cons: I didn't really get jazzed up when I saw him. Also, my mom adored him, so she would probably support the union somewhere deep down under her churchly morals. The other con: Hunter was too emotionally invested for this to be really fun for either of us.

The morning of the party I was assigned the task of decorating the house with small elves and holly. I stuffed plastic holly in every last nook and cranny, until we were festooned with greenery and glowing in the mirth that accompanied Christmas decorations. Then I dropped small crocheted elves in unexpected places around the house—in potted plants, on top of books, peeking out from under the sofa, et cetera. The elf thing was a Bryan family tradition—my mom added a new elf to the collection each year, and my job was to find a clever hiding spot for said addition.

I had run out of creative places to hide the little guys, so many of them were out in the open, which was highly unacceptable to my mom. She hadn't yet learned the all-important lesson in "choosing your battles" and thus didn't realize that by pushing me to get more creative with the preparty elf hiding she was eliminating her opportunity to criticize my party wardrobe selection. That meant I made my big annual debut in slouchy jeans and a reindeer-free sweater. This did not go over well when we posed for the family photo.

By the time the meatballs and cake were laid out in historically gluttonous proportions, the first guests arrived and the festivities could begin. The *glögg* flowed freely, and faces grew red as the sun dropped below the horizon. The field outside our house filled with cars as more and more of the adults from town made the trek out to the boondocks for festivities—no kids from school (Hunter excepted, of course) were dragged to parties like this. I wasn't even able to force Sadie to keep me company, since she was off at her grandparents'.

Mrs. Krapp was back, which meant many of the local ladies were holding their husbands just a bit tighter than they had the year before. The party was in full swing by the time the Johnsons arrived.

I spotted Hunter as he came through the front door, and he looked nervous. He pulled the front of his shirt down over his pleated chinos, hastily surveying the party in search of me. I deliberately hid from him—I don't know why I do these things—and a few minutes later he found me in the kitchen, refilling the meatball dish with a fresh batch that was being kept warm in the Crock-Pot. "Hi, Chaz," he said, his voice hoarse. He cleared his throat.

I was searching for something clever to say when I heard someone around the corner in the living room ask: "How is Chastity handling things?"

My mother responded, "She doesn't know yet. We're afraid of how she'll react—she's so impulsive about these kinds of matters."

"I see." The person, whoever it was, clearly didn't agree with whatever secret my parents were keeping from me. I didn't agree with *any* secrets being kept from me.

"Cancer is such a difficult thing to come to terms with—and she struggles to deal with her emotions," my mom explained. *Cancer?*

"You don't think she'd want to know?"

I'd overheard enough. Still holding the meatball dish, I whipped around the corner into the living room and confronted my mother. She was standing with Mrs. Krapp. "I *would* like to know, actually." Out of respect I chose to keep my voice down so as not to cause a scene at the party. Manners would earn me points I could use later.

My mom was taken aback. Clearly, she hadn't intended for me to hear what she'd been talking about. Maybe she shouldn't have been whispering around the corner from the Crock-Pot. Mrs. Krapp skulked off, plucking a meatball from my dish on her way past. My mom sighed and said, "Oh, Chastity. This isn't a good time."

"Who has cancer, Mom?" I was reeling, and my voice began to shake. "Is there ever a good time for cancer? What do I need to know?"

My dad was standing behind me suddenly, and his arms wrapped around me. I felt his soft belly smush against me as he whispered in my ear, "I do, honey."

The ground fell out from under me as the force of what he'd just told me hit home. Had it not been for my dad standing there hugging me, I may well have crumpled into a pile right there in the living room. That would have proved them right, I guess—a fall would have proved that I "struggle to deal with my emotions."

The magnitude of my parents' words weighed on me as I digested this news. "You have cancer and didn't tell me?" I broke out of the hug and stared at my dad with disbelief, fear and sadness mixed with anger and bitterness. "How long have you known?"

"For about a month," my dad answered quietly. "We didn't want to ruin your Christmas."

I stood there, stunned. "Is it treatable?"

"I hope so." My dad looked sad but not scared. I guess I had missed the whole scared stage. He'd had time to deal with this, to seek comfort from other people, and he'd left me to find out during an overheard conversation at the *kladdkaka* and *köttbullar* party?

"Did you even consider telling me?" I asked. "Were you ever going to tell me, or were you just going to wait until your hair started falling out from the chemo or, God forbid, you *died*? Any chance you considered the fact that I might want to know you were sick?"

My mom put her hand over her mouth and gasped. She started to say something, but my dad cut her off and said, "I chose not to tell you. We never talk about these types of things, and I didn't know how to start the conversation."

His words stung. It was only then that I realized Hunter was standing on the outside of our little group. Seeing an outsider looking in on our family unit made it painfully clear how emotionally stunted we all were—is there any other family in the world that would keep this kind of secret from one another?

I had to get out of there, and I pushed past my parents to my room. When I was safely up the stairs, I let the power of my fear wash over me, and my eyes filled with tears. Heaving sobs, I lay on my bed and curled into a ball.

Cancer: Is a word I've read about, feared, and generally avoided my whole life.

Cancer: Isn't something that happens to my family.

Cancer: This is a big misunderstanding.

When one eavesdrops, one is punished with fear and unnecessary worry, right? I was worried about nothing. No cancer here.

"Chaz, I'm here if you need to talk about it." I hadn't heard Hunter follow me into my room, but there he was, sitting at the end of my bed.

"What are you talking about, Hunter?" I spit this at him, like my tongue was on fire and my breath aflame.

"My aunt went through radiation for breast cancer. I know how you're feeling."

"Oh!" I smiled at him sweetly through the snot-filled tears. "You do?"

He leaned in close, as though we were lovers in love. "I do. And I'm here for you."

"So you've also experienced the feeling of your dad potentially dying but deciding to hide it from you?"

Hunter backed up slightly, afraid. "Chaz, it's okay." He reached out to touch my hair, and my hand instinctively flew up to slap it away. I knew I was acting like a child, but it was unavoidable. If they wanted to treat me like a child, I was more than willing to play the part. "It will help to talk about it."

The way he looked at me, with those deep brown chocolate eyes and his soft, fluffy, dandruff-free hair, made my body and emotions lurch. I was bitter. Bitter about the deception, bitter about my dishonest family, and bitter that my annual holiday party tradition was ruined.

This night was supposed to be about sex. Real sex this time—the sex I deserved after our dress rehearsal last year. Get it on and forget about it. But the way Hunter's eyes shone at me, with so much promise and pity, made me want to hug him or something. It wasn't fair what we were doing here. He was trying to be my knight in shining armor, and I was his fucked-up damsel in distress. That did not make for hot sex—it sounded highly uncomfortable and full of morning-after regret.

"Can you leave, Hunter?"

"Chaz, I want to be here for you. Let me help."

In response I turned away from him and stared at the wall. His eagerness to talk me through the situation and my feelings made me want to seal his mouth with duct tape. This whole scene felt too "relationship" for me, and I couldn't do it.

Couldn't do any of it.

Ours was suddenly a very uneven playing field, and giving Hunter the opportunity to soothe me was surely sending the wrong message. I needed some time to lick my own wounds and deal with the mess of a family I had downstairs. Roping Hunter into the situation wasn't doing anyone any favors. And it appeared that Sadie was right—Hunter and I had very different ideas about where this was all going, and I owed him an out from my fucked-up world.

"I made pancakes!" My mom's voice was inappropriately shiny considering the events of the previous night. I had fallen asleep early—around eight, long before the party was over—so I was up way early for a weekend. Especially for the first Sunday of winter break. Were it not for the fact that my hunger was digging an empty pit in my already nauseous stomach, I would have stayed up in my room until after my parents left for church. But I was famished, so I'd been forced to drag myself downstairs for a family breakfast.

I avoided eye contact and grabbed a bowl from the cabinet. "I'm going to have cereal."

My parents shared a look. "Blueberry pancakes?" My mom was trying so hard.

"I'm gonna go for a run before work." I looked up then,

and their faces were identical pity parties. "I'll puke if I run after pancakes."

"Okay, then," my mom backed off. "So you're working today?"

"This afternoon," I replied. Were we really not going to talk about the *C* word at all? I noticed the kitchen was totally spotless, which meant my parents had stayed up to clean after the party and probably talked about me. I hoped they'd enjoyed that.

"Do you think the restaurant will be busy?" My mom continued with the idle chitchat. It was impressive, actually. How someone could make such a valiant effort at avoiding the tumor in the room was beyond me.

As I spooned up the last of my Cheerios, I finally said, "What kind is it?"

"What's that?" my mom chirped from near the sink.

"What kind of cancer is it?" I was looking directly at my dad, who had been pretending to read the paper. But since it was open to the sports section, I knew he was faking it. He had very limited interest in sports.

He cleared his throat and spoke for the first time that day. "Prostate cancer. It's one of the most common forms of cancer, and very treatable."

"Lucky you." I hated myself for sounding the way I did.

"Chaz." My dad rarely used my nickname, so I knew he was trying to coddle me. "I'm sorry."

"Have you started any kind of treatment yet?"

"Not yet." My dad looked at my mom, who was leaning against the front of the sink, wiping her hands with a dishcloth. The bowl of pancake batter was on the counter next to her, untouched. Clearly, we were all feeling a bit nauseous this morning. "But now that you know . . ."

I looked up, waiting for the second shoe to fall.

My dad looked at my mom, who willingly took over this portion of their script. "Your dad has an appointment with a researcher at the U clinic tomorrow. He's volunteered to be part of a research group with some doctors trying out some new treatment methods. We were going to leave in the morning and be back around dinner, a quick trip there and back, just for the day. But now that you know about all of this, we are considering leaving for Minneapolis tonight. We were thinking about visiting Jeannie and Jack, staying with them." Jeannie is my mom's sister, the rebel of the family (she speaks her mind, which is considered full-on scandal), who we rarely saw.

"Do they know about Dad?" I asked, standing up to put my bowl in the sink.

"Yes." Who else knew? Was I the only person that *didn't* know?

"Well, that sounds fun. You should go early enough that you can go out to dinner tonight. Drive down right after church."

"That *would* be nice." My mom clearly couldn't read the sarcasm in my voice. That was for the best. "Maybe we'll do that. What do you say, Dan?"

My dad was looking at me—I could feel it. He finally said, "Yeah, that sounds good. The Olive Garden or something? Chastity, why don't you come with us? You could spend some time with Alicia?" My cousin Alicia—twelve years old, a total brat. *No thanks.*

"Gotta work." I set my bowl in the top rack of the dishwasher (my mom's pet peeve—she would move it to the bottom as soon as I left the kitchen). "But have fun! I'll hold down the fort here. Call me when you're on your way back."

A few minutes later I was out of the house and off on a ten-mile run that left both my mind and legs numb. I escaped before Mom could bug me about going to church. I had no guilt about that. But I still felt sick and sad for much of my run.

Because I left without telling my dad I loved him.

 THE ONLY THING THAT HAD CHANGED

about Danny Idol since he'd left town was his hairstyle. He had graduated with a modified mullet and now looked like a less-styled Chace Crawford.

I would have rated his looks a solid B on the day he graduated, and he was now an A minus. He was definitely easy to look at, but his personality had not evolved in the least.

When my parents dropped me off at Matt's on their way out of town later that afternoon, Danny was there. He was resting comfortably at the bar, chatting with Matt and a guy

I recognized from the class ahead of Danny. One of Sadie's brother Jeremy's friends, I was pretty sure.

"Hey," Danny greeted me lazily, as though we were old friends. We had been at a few parties together during his years in Milton, but we'd never really hung out or anything.

"Hey," I said back. "Welcome home, fallen Idol."

He laughed at that and looked at Matt. "I like this girl."

"Great," I muttered, ducking under the bar. I grabbed a pen and waited on a group of women who were overly giggly and wore a *Dancing with the Stars* amount of makeup. By the time their stuff was ready, most of the tables were full, and we were impressively busy. Tina Zander came in with a couple of her friends from last year's graduating class—Danny fans— and sat near the bar, flirting and falling all over him when he came out to bus a table.

I was proud of Tina. At least she was coming around to the fact that she had a life beyond Vic.

We hit a lull around eight, and it was only then that I realized Sebastian hadn't been in all night. Angela and I bundled up and went out back for a quick break: her to smoke, me to stretch. "Where's the boy toy tonight?" she asked.

"Yeah . . ." I bent over for a hamstring stretch. Long runs coupled with a shift of waiting tables did a number on the legs. I wanted to lie down and have someone rub my quads.

"Yeah?" Ange prompted. "Boy toy not so cool anymore?" She exhaled, a combination of smoke and steam.

"I don't get him," I said. "He's confusing."

She laughed. "You're confusing." She dropped her cigarette butt on the ground and stamped it out with her foot. She picked the stub up and dropped it in the Dumpster. "What happened?"

"A combination of a whole lot of nothing." I considered my last conversation with Sebastian—Thursday afternoon. "It's weird; one minute it seems like we're sort of flirting, and the next it's like he wants me to get away from him as quickly as possible." Angela shivered in the frozen night air, reminding me that our break was probably over. "Oh, hey!" I said, changing the subject. "My parents are out of town tonight. Want to hang out after you drop me off?"

Her eyes lit up. "Totally. Let's get a group together. Danny's brother will buy us beer, probably."

"Yeah, whatever," I responded as we walked inside through the back door. I wasn't in the mood for a party, but more importantly, I wasn't up for a night alone. Sadie had gone to her grandparents for the weekend for an early Christmas celebration (her parents always wanted to be back in their own house when Santa Claus came to town—apparently the bearded guy only stuffed Sadie's and Jeremy's stockings when he knew where to find them), so I didn't have a lot of options for friends for the night. I didn't want to bother her with my cruddy news during her Christmas festivities, which meant I was holding a lot of anger and self-pity inside myself. With my parents out of town, I was the master of the house, and I felt that deserved a party.

"Maybe he could come?" Angela gestured toward the front door, where Sebastian stood bundled up in his black coat, looking lost.

My heart raced, wondering if he'd come to see me. Maybe I'd overanalyzed the weird end to our last conversation. Maybe he hadn't noticed how awkward the conversation had been between us? I strolled over to the door and gestured toward the PICK A SEAT sign. "It's seat yourself," I teased.

"My table's taken." He was right—a couple was sitting at his usual table, and the only open place was at the bar. A group of guys pushed through the front door just then, and Sebastian reached out to grab my arm and pull me closer to him as they passed. His hands wrapped around my upper arm, and I could smell his cinnamon gum. He leaned his face down, close to mine, and said, "I didn't come for food."

My breath caught in my throat. When I looked up, the first thing I noticed was that he had one blue eye and one brown one, and they were both searching my eyes intently.

Our faces were mere inches apart again. I wanted to lift up on my toes and close the gap, but instead I said, "I'm having some people over to my house tonight. You must be bored. Come."

He laughed and let my arm drop. We were alone in the entryway again, and there was no need for us to be this close. No need, except that I *wanted* to be this close to him. It felt like someone turned my body from "off" to "on" when he was in the room. The feeling was totally foreign. So new, so liberating. "Yeah, maybe."

"Maybe?" I was surprised. It must have been the way he laughed when I asked, but I'd thought he'd say no for sure. "Cool—do you have a car?"

"I can borrow my dad's." I told him how to get to my house and said we'd be there sometime around eleven thirty. We exchanged cell numbers, just in case. "Maybe I'll see you then," he said.

"Maybe." And then he left.

Wolf smells like kitty litter. I obsessed over that thought while I was squished next to him in Angela's car on our way to my house later that night. I don't have cats and don't want cats, and part of the reason for that is that the smell of kitty litter makes me want to ralph. Thus Wolf makes me want to ralph.

"Do you have cats?" I asked, masking my mouth a little,

since I'd eaten a burger with fried onions on my break (without thinking that plan through properly) and I didn't want my breath steaming over kitty litter–scented Wolf. I didn't need to give him a reason to have something against me in the odor department.

He put his arm around me, as though a slight discussion about cats were a come-on or something. Furry creatures equal sex. . . . I thought of the humping bunnies Sadie and I had watched on Animal Planet last weekend and squirmed away from him. "Yeah, I've got four. Want to come over and meet them?" He leered toward me, and my fried onions lurched crudely amongst my stomach juices.

"I'll take a pass on that, Wolf. Ange, can you drive faster?" She looked at me in the rearview mirror, her eyes watery crescent moons beneath her driving glasses. "No?" I queried, glancing at Wolf. "I'll deal."

By the time we got to my house, I was tempted to shower. Though we'd worked together for a year and a half, I'd never really gotten that physically close to Wolf before, and now I knew why. I couldn't understand how Angela could have suspended her gag reflex long enough to have actually gotten it on with him.

We were the first of three cars to arrive at my place. Ange had taken me, Wolf, and Ryan (her dish boy), all squeezed into the backseat. Angela's front seat was missing a pad, so to sit shotgun meant settling your cheeks on just the metal seat framing. I might have been willing to do that if I'd realized how vile Wolf was prior to the ride.

The second car had the booze. Danny Idol, his brother, and some guy named Matthew who went to college with Danny's brother were obvious invites to our little shindig, considering the fact that Danny's brother, Alan, was twenty-one. They were older guys, which made it weird that they were hanging out with us, but since Matthew wore dorky square glasses and a scarf, I jumped to conclusions and assumed he was safe.

The third car carried Tina Zander, Kristy Wilton, Morgan Vandersall, and Harmony Brines, who had been hanging out at Matt's all night, keeping an eye on Danny. Tina and Kristy are in my class, and Morgan and Harmony had graduated with Danny the year before. They had all come over because of Danny Idol, not because of me. Tina was pretending we were all buddy-buddy, but I knew that was just because she wanted Danny to think she was Little Miss Popular.

I made everyone go straight downstairs when we got there, then grabbed a few leftover holiday party goods from the fridge for people to nosh on. Danny and Alan carried in the beer, and people settled into my big L-couch and turned on the TV. Angela and Ryan snuck up to the living room almost immediately, and when I went upstairs to get a roll of paper towels to wipe up Tina's beer spill, I could hear them panting on the floor. It was totally grode, but considering the fact that both Ange and Ryan still lived with their parents, they were probably going nuts about being out of their family prison, free to get it on wherever and whenever, for the night.

We'd been there for almost half an hour, and I'd given up on Sebastian. It was close to midnight, and I assumed there was no way he'd show up at that hour. His dad must have gotten home from work hours ago, and really, what parent would let their kid drive out to the middle of nowhere to hang out at a total stranger's house? When the doorbell rang about four seconds later, I realized Sebastian's dad must be the kind of parent who was cool about that, and I loved him for it.

I answered the door quickly—I'd just finished brushing my teeth (those fried onions), so was on my way down from the bathroom when he showed up. "Hi!" I exclaimed, opening the door. "You came."

"Maybe," he replied. Then he smiled, and the world spun away, leaving just me and him and a pocketful of fantasies. He broke the mood I was trying to set with my eyes when he whispered, "Do you have a dog?"

"What? No."

"What's that panting?"

I laughed. "That's just Angela and Ryan. They're horny."

"Right," he said, nodding. "What kind of party is this?"

He amused me. I led him downstairs to introduce him around. It was strange, introducing this guy I hardly knew to a bunch of other people I hardly knew. By virtue of the fact that I was the host of the party, there was some assumption that I was the thread that united everyone. But in fact the beer was the unifying thread here, and I was simply providing a venue for consumption of said thread.

They were watching some horror flick, and the couch was too full for us to squeeze in, which I wasn't sad about. Kristy and Tina had both nuzzled up against Danny to shield them from the meanies on the TV, and Morgan and Harmony were both watching enviously as he faux-scared each of the girls hanging off of him by periodically shouting "boo." I could tell from their reactions that they were totally faking it to up their cuteness factor.

Alan and Matthew looked bored, but they were only partially through their beers, so it seemed like they were stuck for a little while longer watching Danny charm the ladies with his mad skilz. Wolf was working the leftover girls, but no one seemed interested. Judging from the empties on the table, Wolf was on beer number three. That wasn't helping his odds any.

The introductions were quick, and then Sebastian and I settled into beanbag chairs around the corner from the TV. I could smell cinnamon gum again and realized it must be his thing. I knew I would never smell cinnamon gum again without picturing his gorgeous smile.

"Do you want a beer or anything?" I offered, over in our quiet corner of the room. As he got comfortable in his beanbag, I couldn't help but notice that his jeans were kinda tight and came in at the bottom—this forced me to take a quick peek at the other guys on the couch, all of whom were still sporting the baggy-jeans style. I'd always thought tightish jeans on a guy were a little weird and feminine, but I guess it said something about his body confidence. That wouldn't hurt when it came to the getting it on portion of our evening (...if I was lucky).

"No, thanks. I'm not much of a drinker."

"Me either."

"You're just an enabler?"

"Because I let them all hang here?" I pushed my hair away from my face. "Yeah, I guess so. But I didn't buy the beer, so I'm totally innocent."

"I doubt that," he said, making my heart skip a beat. He readjusted on the beanbag, which made me worry about his comfort level.

"Do you want to go upstairs or something?" I offered.

"See what I mean?" he laughed. "Not so innocent."

"That's totally not what I meant." *Okay, I guess it was. Subconsciously.*

"Uh-huh."

We just sat there then, saying nothing. I was mildly freaking out because he'd rejected what he'd perceived to be an attempted come-on. Was he just not interested in me? After a long silence I finally said, "Are you as bored in Milton as the rest of us?"

He leaned his head back against the wall and turned to look at me. The skin under his chin looked so yummy, so kissable, that I wanted to reach over and touch it. He had soft-looking skin that had a thin layer of hair growth. I wanted to rub it and see if it was downy or prickly. "Not really," he admitted. "It's not bad, I guess."

"You must miss your friends."

He looked away from me then, staring up at the ceiling when he answered. "I'm surviving." We sat there silently for a few minutes, listening to the gory screams from the TV around the corner and Danny's ridiculous flirting. "It's cool spending some time with my dad. You probably don't get this, but it's weird for me to live with just my mom all the time. She's cool, but I guess I didn't realize what a difference the guy vibe makes around the house."

"I totally get it," I said, mirroring his position against the wall. We were both staring up at the ceiling, but still conversing with one another—two planets on the same orbital path. "I would be a wreck if it were just me and my mom. My dad's the only person who's somewhat normal around here." I considered this statement, as I remembered the events of the previous night. *Would a normal dad hide cancer from his daughter?*

"Are your parents gone?"

"Yeah," I answered. "Thus the beer."

He laughed. "I guess."

"So it's just you and your mom, all the time?" I asked, wondering if I was prying too hard. I hadn't really expected that this was how we'd spend our night. Just chatting.

He glanced over, and I saw that his eyes were an open door again, sort of the way they'd been the other night at Matt's, before he'd closed the emotional shutters over them when I'd stuck my fat foot in my mouth. "Yep. Me and Jenny."

"Who's Jenny?" I asked. *Sister? Girlfriend?*

"My mom."

"Right. Jenny." I paused for what felt like an appropriate amount of time, both of us resuming our eyes-on-the-ceiling positions, then asked, "And your girlfriend?"

He looked at me again with that melty, sensual, sexpot stare. "What makes you think there's a girlfriend?"

I paused, trying to figure out if I should play this like Tina Zander would, or if I should give him an introduction to Chastity Bryan 101. I voted for me. "Because I've given you every sign I'm interested, and you're a little, um, distant. I guess I figured we'd be hooking up in my room by now, not sitting three feet apart in these moldy beanbags." I said this lightly, hoping it was obvious I wasn't some sort of creep or desperate loser—but I was confident I'd made my intentions clear.

"Wouldn't that make me sort of an asshole?"

"Not necessarily." I shrugged. "Depends on the girl you ask. Some girls are only looking for one thing, deep down— and it's not always love with a chance of marriage."

He looked back up at the ceiling, so I couldn't see his eyes, but I could sense the shift in him, could tell the shutters were closing back up. "Don't take this the wrong way," he said, which meant I would most certainly take it the wrong way. "But I'm not really looking for that right now. I think you're totally cool, but I need to keep this—"

"It's fine." I cut him off. I didn't need to hear more.

"You wouldn't understand."

"Probably not." I smiled at him to show him there were no hard feelings. Even though there were. But I still liked talking to him, and I was discovering there was something very relax-ing about being around him. I also found it very comforting that he was an outsider, someone who would be gone after winter break, someone who wasn't analyzing me with their Milton glasses on. Someone who couldn't get too close.

"It's just . . ." He squeezed his hand into a fist and growled slightly. It was very animalistic and turned me on even more. *Freaking tease*, I thought. "I think you're so hot, and you seem cool, but I just . . . can't."

"You can't or you won't?" I was enjoying the game.

"I can't. And I should really go," he said, without moving at all.

"Okay."

"Can we hang out again?" He was being too gentlemanly. It didn't suit him, so I knew he was playing my game, hiding the truth behind the veneer, at least a little bit. "When are you working next?"

"Tuesday afternoon."

"I'll come in," he promised.

I laughed. "Maybe I'll see you then."

He grinned, sending shudders down my spine. "Maybe."

And then he was gone.

**MONDAY MORNING, WAY TOO EARLY,**

I went over to Sadie's. I knew she was getting back from her grandparents late Sunday night, since her folks had to work. Thank God for that—I needed her clear logic and good advice more than I ever had. Though it killed me, I was forced to take the snowmobile. We had gotten about six inches overnight, and the car wouldn't start, but my rural ass had to get into town somehow.

I knew she'd still be asleep when I got there, so I just let myself in the house (locks aren't necessary in Milton) and walked through to her room in the back. I climbed into bed next to her and lay there silently, waiting for her to wake up. I knew it was a little creepy. Sadie had come to expect this sort of thing from me, though, so I hoped she wouldn't be too freaked when she opened her eyes and found me next to her.

"Ayeeeee!" Sadie's eyes popped open, and she sat upright.

"Sorry," I muttered. "You didn't know I was here?"

"Gosh, Chaz, you scared the bejeezus out of me." She rubbed her eyes and looked at the clock. "It's not even nine."

"Not to be dramatic," I said apologetically, "but my life literally fell apart while you were opening presents with your grandma."

Sadie had lain back down and pulled her duvet up under her chin. "Is Sebastian still being mean to you?" she teased.

"Sebastian is actually not being mean to me." I swallowed, bracing myself. "Sadie, it's really bad." I then went into every last detail from the party on Saturday night, starting with the cancer secret and ending with my awkward family breakfast on Sunday morning. By the time I finished telling her everything, I was in tears, and Sadie was hugging me, and I finally felt like I could let go of a lot of the things that had been stuck inside since Saturday night.

"You could have called me." Sadie brushed my hair back

from my face, looking at me with her sweet, innocent eyes and reminding me how lucky I was to have a friend like her.

"I know," I blubbered. "It was sort of nice to have a couple days to be angry and bitchy about it before I had to be rational. But I'm glad you're back."

"Does your dad seem sick?" she asked gently.

"No," I admitted. "Honestly, he just seems old and fat."

She laughed. That had been my intention. "Does he have to have chemo?"

"I don't know. My parents left yesterday to go to Minneapolis to meet with some doctors. They get back tonight."

"Wow."

"Yeah, wow." And that was the moment when I turned something off again. That little switch that tells my emotions to hold back, the same one that instructs my mouth to keep itself zipped up when the conversation turns to me. I don't mean to do it, but whenever a conversation starts digging in too deep, I start piling the sand back on, covering up my emotional privates. "Oh, hey, did Trav give you his Christmas present yet?"

Sadie allowed the abrupt switch in the conversation and happily bubbled on about her Christmas plans with Trav for Thursday night, the eve of Christmas Eve. They were going to exchange presents then, and probably some bodily fluids, too.

She didn't say that last bit, but I did a little internal editorializing. "I hope he doesn't get me clothes," Sadie said, giggling. "I've been so famished after that stomach bug that I've literally been eating every Christmas cookie in sight. I'm on a junk food warpath or something."

"You look better." I had started to worry about her, but the cookies had obviously started to bring some of the flush and fullness back to her cheeks. She was looking much more like the rounded, squeezable Sadie I loved. "Your boobs look huge in those pj's."

We lay around for an hour, talking only a little more about my dad; then I surfed the Web while she took a shower and put on her makeup. When she was finally ready to go, the realization that we had nowhere to go finally hit us. It was Christmas break, and we had absolutely nothing to do. "Wanna go shopping?" Sadie suggested.

I gagged. "I guess."

"You have a car?"

"Broken again. I've got the love machine out back."

We looked at each other. The only mall—and it was a shabby half mall—was in Flanders, and I for one was not hauling myself there via snowmobile. Fast-moving crisp air was not my thing. Sadie finally said, "We could call Jen or Tegan. They always like shopping, and one of them can get a car."

"I guess." I shrugged. I wasn't in the mood for Jen or Tegan—but I needed something to do, and shopping was definitely distracting. Maybe I could sneak off and see a movie while the other girls looked for clothes. "Yeah, call Jen."

"They're picking us up in fifteen," Sadie announced when she got off the phone.

I smiled. I had to keep a happy face on, or Sadie would bring my dad up again. I didn't really feel like talking about it anymore, and I certainly didn't want to discuss it with Jen in the car. If I wasn't comfortable baring all for Sadie, I certainly wasn't going to spill my beans with a partial stranger. "Great. This will be fun."

When Jen pulled up a little while later, Sadie bounced out to the car. I slipped into the backseat and immediately realized that Tina Zander was sitting in the front passenger seat next to Jen. I guess I'd always assumed Jen and Tegan went everywhere together and didn't really branch out to hang with other people. So it surprised me to see Tina there and *not* Tegan. Maybe I hadn't been paying close enough attention to the social network lately.

"Hey," Tina said, flashing me a genuine smile. "Thanks for having us over last night."

Sadie looked at me—I'd failed to mention the party to her. I smiled back at Tina. "Yeah, no problem. It was fun."

"Who's that Sebastian guy?" Tina queried, warmer than usual. Now that she had a possible love affair with Danny Idol on the back burner, she seemed less threatened by me with Vic. *Go, Tina.* "He's *cuuuuute*."

Sadie was staring at me now. "He's just this guy," I explained to Tina and Jen. I looked at Sadie and said, "Tina hung out at my place with some of the Matt's crew last night—Sebastian came over too. Later, though. He didn't stay long."

She narrowed her eyes at me. "Interesting . . ."

"Not really," I confessed. "Sebastian's an enigma."

"Ew," Tina whined. "That sounds gross. What's a nigma?" God, did she and Vic make a cute couple. There could be no better match.

I ignored her and kept talking to Sadie. "There's no potential. He made that very clear."

"Maybe he's gay?" Sadie suggested.

"Nuh-uh!" Tina's comments from the front seat were a fun addition to the conversation.

"Nope," I declared. "He said this weird thing that made me think he was interested, but not . . . but I definitely get the sense he's into girls."

"Thank God for that!" Tina again. She looked back to raise her eyebrows at me. "Milton doesn't need any freaks."

"Nice, Tina." I shot her a *shut the fuck up* look but chose not to counter with the comment that Milton was already full of freaks—it's just that the people I would consider freaks are far different from the people Tina would call freaks. It was a matter of perspective, and I knew my perspective was probably in the minority in my town. It wasn't worth a verbal battle with Tina on this one.

"Did he try to kiss you?" Sadie wiggled her eyebrows.

Jen glanced at me in the rearview. I shook my head. "Most definitely not." I wanted to turn this conversation train away from me, so I said, "What are you guys doing for Christmas?"

This led us down a nice long path that gave Tina the stage for the majority of the drive. She talked about how her cat has this cute Santa hat, and the family dresses up and takes a super funny picture where they're all posed around the cat, with the hat, stuffed inside a Christmas stocking that they hang from the mantle.

When we finally got to the mall, I was relieved to have the merry sounds of the season drown out Tina's yammering for a while. Flanders Mall is a big draw for a lot of small towns in Northern Minnesota, so mall management goes all out when it comes to holidays. Santa's North Pole stretched almost the entire main corridor length (which wasn't very long), and fake snow was hanging from every beam and storefront.

There were actually live reindeer in a cage on the west side of the mall. We stayed far from there, since the only store in that area was the Dress Barn, and the proximity to the reindeer meant it smelled like an actual barn.

Sadie, in a true best friend move, made up some lie about how she needed me to consult on a present for Trav or something, and could we meet up with the other girls later? I shot her a grateful look as we walked away, arm in arm. "Sebastian was seriously at your house last night? He came over—that's gotta mean something."

"It doesn't." I told her about his "I think you're hot" line and his growl and the fist and how it would never happen. "So I'm trying to let it go."

She pulled me into the bookstore, on a quest for some ice fishing book for Trav. "I don't know, Chaz."

"Trust me." I grabbed a book called *Are You Ready for College?* and flipped to the end to see what the answer was. "I opened the door really wide and invited him in, and he passed. I couldn't have been more obvious, even if I'd gotten naked and stood in front of him with a little bow tied around my waist."

"Chaz! What's wrong with you?" Sadie darted over and put her hand across my mouth. I licked her hand and she pulled it away again. "You're disgusting."

I laughed. "I'm just saying I pretty much sat on his lap

and he still said no. I don't need to act desperate. I'm not Tina Zander." This last thing I said quietly, since you never know who might overhear. I didn't need to wage that war.

"Fine." Sadie pursed her lips. "I get it." She was trying hard not to smile.

"What about this for Trav?" I offered her a book entitled *Tantric Sex and You*.

Sadie hastily grabbed it from me and stuffed it on a shelf with cookbooks. "I'm good. Thanks." She bought her copy of *The (N)Ice Fisherman* while I kept shuffling through the college readiness book.

"Have you heard from the U yet?" she asked as we walked out the door. "I think Carissa Jackson got her acceptance last week."

I acted surprised—I had heard about Carissa, too, which meant University of Minnesota acceptances were being sent out, and it would be a lot harder to hide my lie about not having yet applied. "No, nothing yet."

"I was looking through the Macalester course catalog at my grandma's. There's a class called Women, Gender, and Sexuality—maybe they have the same sort of thing at the U? You'd like that, I'm sure."

"Yeah. Maybe."

"I'm thinking about majoring in architecture. There's this

really cool thing where you stay at Macalester for the first three years, then go to St. Louis and do architecture at Washington University. How crazy would it be if I moved to St. Louis?" She beamed at me. "I mean, I wouldn't go forever or anything. I'm sure I'll move back home, but it's fun to think about."

"How do you know you'd move back home?"

"I don't know." Sadie chewed her fingernail. "I guess I just always assumed that's what I would do. I mean, maybe I could live in Flanders or something."

"Or New York. If you want to do architecture, that's where you should go, right?"

Sadie giggled. "New York? I don't think so."

"You could."

"No." Sadie dismissed me easily, as though the thought had never crossed her mind. I realized we never had discussed our longer-term visions in any real detail—it had been about college and then . . . nothing. Had she really never envisioned a future for herself anywhere but here? Was I really that foreign in my own hometown? And why was my own future still so fuzzy?

I decided I needed to tell her. My life was suddenly full of too many secrets, and it was crazy that I couldn't even be honest with my best friend about *college*, of all things. Sure, Sadie had her life planned out, and her future was perfectly mapped . . . but that didn't mean she'd be critical of me for not knowing where I was going to take my life next. I mean, a ton of people in my town weren't going to college right away, if at all, and that wasn't weird. Why was I keeping this big, unimpressive secret bundled up inside? "Sade, I have to tell you something—"

"Hey, girls!" That was Tina, hollering from inside the manicure place. She was fanning her red and green painted nails at us.

"Yeah?" Sadie prompted, responding to my comment. "What were you going to say?"

I grinned casually, the moment lost. "Oh, just that—" I cut off, looking for something to say to prove it had been nothing. "My Christmas gift to you is a manicure!" *What?* Where had that come from? *Gack.*

Sadie looked thrilled. "Really? Seriously, Chaz?"

"Merry Christmas."

 **■ MY PARENTS GOT HOME LATE MONDAY**
night, about twenty minutes after I'd crawled into bed. I
heard them come in but closed my blanket over my head
and pretended to be asleep. I didn't want to hear about the
treatment, didn't want to hear how things went. Clearly, I
wasn't a part of this process, so why try to insert myself now?

When I woke in the morning, it was early. I deliberately
lay in bed until I heard them leave to drop my dad off at work.
I knew I had some time before my mom would be back with
the car, so I luxuriated in a long shower and thought about

how today might be the day Sebastian would be coming into Matt's to see me.

I found a note on the counter when I went downstairs. After pouring a bowl of cereal, I sat down to read it:

Chastity:

1. *Tanner is coming by this morning to look at the car. Take some money out of my drawer to pay him.*
2. *I've asked Hunter to come by the restaurant today to see you—you need a friend right now that you can talk to about everything.*
3. *We're having Christmas Eve dinner with the Johnsons. Please make sure you have the night off so we can be a proper family.*
4. *Clean the bathroom before work.*

PS: Your father's appointment went well. There's nothing for you to worry about.

It was a PS. My dad had cancer, and all it warranted was a PS in my mom's list of instructions.

Looking back over the list, I sighed. On a positive note the car would be fixed, so I wouldn't have to rely on my mom or figure out another ride in to work. On the flip side, however, I had two dates with Hunter arranged on my calendar.

He was coming to Matt's today? My mom thought Hunter would be the best person for me to talk to? Not, um, my best friend? Had she really arranged a setup at my place of employment? Did she think we would fall in love over discussions of my dad's cancer? Agh.

Christmas Eve with the Johnsons—hip hip hooray! We were going to be a family united in love and in Christ. It was truly meant to be.

Three hours into my shift Sebastian still hadn't been by. I started work at noon—Tanner had replaced the battery in the car with one he'd rescued from the junkyard in Flanders, so I'd been able to drive myself—and it was now three, and the place was dead quiet. I was the only waitress working. Angela started at four, so we overlapped for an hour. But at this rate I'd be sent home as soon as Ange got there.

"What are you doing for Christmas?" Matt asked me through the kitchen peek-through. "Big plans?"

"Nah, just the usual." I remembered my mom's list, and her instruction about Christmas Eve. "Hey, do you need some extra help on Christmas Eve?"

"I'm going to close up early that night. Take some time off before the day after Christmas hits." Matt was cleaning off ketchup bottles, and I gagged a little when his fingernail flicked a piece of goobed-up ketchup into his face. "How was the party at your place the other night?"

I thought back to that night, to my time with Sebastian. He was strange and such a mystery to me—what was his deal? "It was fun. Danny's a trip."

Matt laughed. "He's a good kid."

"I don't deny that," I agreed. "He's a hottie, too."

"Not you, Chaz!" Matt gawked at me. "You have better taste than Danny."

Matt was so gullible and dorky. "Yeah, Danny's not really my thing. But that doesn't mean he's not hot."

The front door opened, and I snapped to attention. I was too excited to see Sebastian to pretend to be cool about it. But it was just Danny, arriving a little early for his shift. "Speak of the Idol," I muttered to Matt.

Danny settled in at the bar and knocked on it to announce his readiness for a drink. "Coke, please, pretty lady."

"Get it yourself." I grinned. "I'm busy."

Matt shrugged at Danny. "You heard the girl. She's busy. We're busy." Matt looked at me for support, then announced to Danny, "Get your own darn pop."

"Chastity's charm is rubbing off on you, eh, Matt?" He stood up and poured himself a big plastic cup full of pop from the soda fountain. "What you been up to this morning?"

I didn't get a chance to answer, since the door opened again just then, and my insides took a tumble when I assumed it would finally be Sebastian. But when I looked up, Hunter was standing there, in all his fluffy-haired glory. He looked at me shyly, then took a seat at the far end of the bar, as far from Danny as possible. Cute, confident boys threatened him. "What up?" Danny called, flashing a grin at Hunter. Danny took every opportunity for self-promotion, always looking for a new fan.

Hunter waved awkwardly. I lazily dragged myself over to him and offered him a drink. "How's it going?"

"How are you?" he asked meaningfully. He was taking his role as my Mom-directed confidant very seriously. "I've been thinking of you."

Great, I thought. *This is getting more unbalanced by the second.* Out loud I said, "In what way?"

"What's that?" Hunter took a swig of the Coke I'd just put in front of him.

"In what way have you been thinking of me?"

"About, well, I've been thinking about your dad. How are you coping?"

"That's what you're thinking about when you're thinking about me? Are you sure?"

"Chaz . . ." He was gearing up to reprimand me. I could feel it. "Be serious for a minute. I want to help you. I'm here to talk about it."

"This is just the place I want to talk about it," I whispered sarcastically. "I appreciate the fact that my mom sent you here and you feel obligated to do her bidding, but maybe *I don't want to talk about this with you.*"

Hunter swallowed—his Adam's apple bobbed deeply in his throat. He was nervous. I was scaring him. Good. "That's fine too. We can talk about something else. But just know I'm here for you."

"Great." I faked a giant smile. "That means so much to me."

"Come on, Chastity," he urged quietly. "Let someone in."

What the fuck? Again with the emotionally closed-off criticism? I was sensing a theme. "You want in, Hunter?" I narrowed my eyes at him.

Matt came out from the back and interrupted. "Hey, Chaz, you're cut, okay? I can cover things here—Ange will be here soon, and Danny can always wait tables if we need extra help."

I felt sick, realizing that my Tuesday shift was about to end and Sebastian hadn't shown up like he'd promised. I really thought he'd come. Hunter had come instead. "I can hang around, Matt," I offered weakly. "I don't mind."

"There's no sense in you standing here for the next hour. Enjoy the afternoon."

"Okay." I thanked him and dropped my apron behind the counter. I headed toward the door, waiting for Hunter to follow. My dad had his long shift at work on Tuesdays, and Mom was at choir rehearsal, so I had the house to myself for a couple more hours. "Are you coming?" Hunter just sat at the bar, lamely waiting for a handwritten invite or something. "You said you wanted in, right?"

He hopped up. "Are you going home?"

"Yeah," I said. I had a veneer of confidence melted over my body, but internally I was seething and sad. Why did I feel so disappointed with my life? Had Sebastian really had such a significant effect on me that I was depressed and sulking about him not showing up? That was messed up, and I knew what I had to do take back control. I raised my eyebrows at Hunter. "Coming?"

He looked at me, and I saw him realize what I was saying. "You want me to come home with you?" I couldn't tell what he was thinking, and I suddenly didn't care. I just wanted to make him stop looking at me with that horrible, pitiful look.

"Come if you want." I pushed through the back door

and climbed into my car. Hunter still wasn't my top choice, but Sebastian was clearly a nonoption, and I'd been robbed of my opportunity with Hunter at the holiday party. I was owed a do-over. I needed a release, and Hunter provided a safe escape—a chance for me to let go.

He climbed into his car and followed me home. I hoped he would finally understand what I needed him for.

The way my body felt when Hunter and I stepped into my house was alarmingly familiar. I felt the same numb desire I'd felt the first time we'd had sex, and I knew this probably wasn't the best idea. At the time I didn't quite know *why* it wasn't the best idea, but there was something blandly irritating somewhere under my skin that made me feel icky. It was almost like that feeling of having a pebble in your shoe, the kind that's so small it's not worth stopping to take your shoe off for, and then when you get home the pebble has rubbed against your skin in such a way all afternoon that you have a blister.

I guess that made my relationship with Hunter like a blister.

But the blister hadn't yet begun to form—it was just a feeling inside that made me the tiniest bit uncomfortable while he was tugging off my Matt's T-shirt. His lips were cold and overly damp as he laid kisses on my body. I just lay there, staring up at the ceiling in the basement, wondering if there was anything good on TV. Anything that would make me feel more in the mood for this. More in the mood for him to be my boyfriend—isn't that what I was supposed to want?

Get over it, I scolded myself. Then, without thinking, I grabbed the remote from the floor next to me with one hand and hit the power button. I was so quick with my mute finger that Hunter didn't even know what was going on over his shoulder. *Who Wants to Be a Millionaire?* Shit. That wasn't worth risking him seeing what I was doing while we did what we were about to do. I flipped the TV back off and tried to get into it. I thought of Sebastian, and at that moment my body responded to Hunter in the way it should. But the bliss only lasted seconds, and then I was back—in my basement, with Hunter Johnson.

I really wanted to be excited about this. Truly. Everything about Hunter suggested he was a good choice for me. He was nice; he was decent-looking; he was good to my parents; he was supportive. But he didn't incite that fire that made my belly ache and my body scream. *Is this what I will settle for?* I wondered, as he delicately sucked my earlobe. *Is this my future? Sufficient sex with a halfway decent guy?*

Hunter reached his hand down my body, gripping at the top of my jeans before reaching inside. His arm stretched down, on a quest for something specific, some secret place he wanted to explore. He was on top of me now, so his arm was caught awkwardly between our bodies as he tried to maneuver into position.

My shirt was pulled up, so my back was exposed, and my skin rubbed against the carpet. Every time Hunter squirmed on top of me, my body shifted and the carpet dug into my skin. It was starting to burn. I distracted myself by reaching down to unsnap his fly, and I eased his zipper down. His pants flapped open, and I saw that he was wearing Green Bay Packers boxers. *Traitor*, I thought. *This is Vikings country.*

His breath was coming in shorter bursts now, and he moaned when I pulled my own jeans down around my knees. I kicked one foot free, my jeans hanging on around one leg. Hunter tugged at my underwear eagerly. He began to rub against me.

This is it, I thought, as his body pushed against mine. There was only one thin layer of clothes left, and we'd be back in business. *Sex with Hunter, take two.*

And then, suddenly, he stopped. "What the fuck?" he said breathlessly.

"What's wrong?" I asked, pulling him back against me.

"Your grandma." He was looking up, staring disgustedly toward the TV. "She's watching us."

I craned my neck around, looking at Nonna's picture and the rosary beads draped around her frame. "Do you want me to cover the picture up?" I offered, knowing full well that the moment had been ruined already.

"I can't do this, Chaz."

"You can." I reached down and felt him, still hard inside his boxers. "You know you want to." I felt like a pusher—some creepy drug dealer who preys on unsuspecting kids. I was making myself sick. "I want you."

"You don't want me," he said sadly. "You're willing to have sex with me, but you don't really want me."

I sat up, tugging my underwear back into place before pulling my jeans back on. I didn't know what to say, so Hunter spoke again. "It's not about sex or hooking up or whatever—this is real for me, Chastity." His shoulders were hunched, and he didn't look at me when he said, "I love you."

It's funny how at this point in movies the girl finally realizes that she's been fawning over the wrong guy and that the *right* guy has been in front of her the whole time. With those three little words that Hunter had just said, movie girls realize their wrongs and recognize their golden future with the boy they hadn't really noticed until that magical moment. That realization didn't happen for me.

"I know," was all I said back. He looked at me hopefully,

wondering if there was anything more coming. The numbness continued to spread inside of me, and I could only say, "I'm sorry."

In less than two minutes Hunter was out of there. I knew I'd broken his heart, and I did feel bad about that. But I couldn't settle—wouldn't settle—and without the spark there would be no hope for us.

Did I wish I could feel something for Hunter? Maybe.

Did I feel guilty that I'd let my own fucked-up emotions and single-minded drive for sex dick Hunter over? Absolutely.

Was I holding out for more than I could get? Probably.

Was it worth it? I hoped so.

**11.** **AS SOON AS I HEARD HUNTER'S CAR**

start and the rumble of tires on salted gravel, I grabbed my cell and dialed Sebastian. Screw the fact that he hadn't shown up at Matt's—I didn't need to wait for him to tell me I could talk to him. I was allowed to make the next move.

Sebastian answered right away and told me to come over, so I ran upstairs to rinse off my face and then jumped in the car. I drove slowly in the snow, since my rural road was last on the plow and salt-truck route.

His house was even smaller than I remembered, a tiny

shacklike thing that sunk into its lot. The snow piled up around the perimeter made it look half buried.

I climbed up the concrete front porch steps and lifted my hand to ring the bell. Sebastian pulled the door open, and his face lit up with that cocky, sexy smile that had haunted me since he'd first rolled into town. "Hey, party girl."

"Hi, table six."

"Come on in." I paused on the stoop. He caught my hesitation and said, "My dad's working."

"Okay." The house was sparse. The living room (tiny) had a really strange furniture setup, with the front of the couch pushed up against the big picture window so you couldn't even sit on it normally. There were two wooden rocking chairs facing a TV propped up on a TV tray, and a little café table in the corner (apparently the dining room). The miniature, one-person-only kitchen was visible through a cutout wall in the middle of the living room, and I could see there were dirty dishes piled in the sink.

There was a little hallway that, I imagined, led away from the living room to the bedrooms and bathroom. And that was it. We stood in the middle of the living room for a few seconds.

"Do you want something to drink?"

"Um, sure. What do you have?"

"Water."

"Sparkling?" I don't even like sparkling water—who knows why I thought this would be funny.

"Milton's finest," he answered. "Plain old tap water."

"Great—water it is."

While he filled my glass in the kitchen, he talked to me through the hole in the living room wall. I continued to stand in the middle of the room, hands stuffed in my jeans pockets. "Wouldn't you have guessed that we don't have a wide selection of beverages? Have you noticed that I eat out every day?"

"Every day except today," I replied, immediately addressing the fact that he hadn't shown up. I was allowed to play games, but I had every intention of calling his whenever I spotted a classic playing-hard-to-get move.

He looked pissed as he turned off the water. "I thought you were working today."

Great. So he'd deliberately not come into Matt's because I was working? What did he have against me, and why had he invited me over now? "Yeah," I said. "I was."

"So you got my message?"

"Huh?"

"I went to Matt's, like, half an hour ago—I told that guy Danny to let you know I'd stopped by." Sebastian returned to the living room with my water. I took it from him, and his hand brushed mine during the handoff. Icy shards shot through my wrist and almost made me drop the glass. I had it bad. "I thought that was why you'd called."

"I got cut an hour ago—you showed up?" My heart was melting into this little pool of sweet, gooey lust that sickened me the same way Peeps do at Easter. He had come to see me!

"Yeah," he said. "I wanted a cheeseburger."

Right when he said that, the simplicity of someone like Vic or the sweetness of someone like Hunter became somewhat alluring for the first time ever. Sebastian was a "nigma," and I was all tangled up in his sticky web. I knew it was dangerous to be so twisted up into him, but I was stuck. "A cheeseburger, huh? Did you get what you wanted?"

His face morphed into that smile again, like he was teasing me. His dark hair draped across his forehead, and I wanted to wrap my fingers up in it. "I guess." He was doing this weird thing as he looked at me, where he'd study my eyes, then let his gaze drift down to my mouth when I started talking. It made me want to keep talking, to watch him watching my mouth. "Do you want to sit down?"

"Okay." I looked around, wondering where we were expected to sit. Sebastian moved toward the couch, where he climbed up and over the side of the couch to lie down with his legs dangling over the arm. His head was in the center of the couch, and there was room for me to lay the same way on the other side, with my head touching his in the middle. I set my water on the window ledge and followed his lead. When I was settled, the tops of our heads were lightly touching, but our bodies were going off in different directions. "This is very strange," I admitted.

"Yeah," he agreed, with no further comment.

"Do you always have your couch like this?"

"Pushed up against the window?" I nodded, but he couldn't see it. "Not always—but today."

"Any reason why?"

He laughed. "You're pushy." There was a pause before he explained. "I shoved it up against the window so I could lie here and look up and see the snow. It's a pretty view, all snowy and drifty like this."

"Makes sense." It did make sense. The big picture window at the front of the house was wide and expansive, and when I lay like this on the couch and looked up, I could see the sky and the trees and the tiny little icicles on the eaves. It almost felt like lying on the ground, looking up at the sky, but we were sheltered inside. "I like it."

"I do too. It makes me feel like I'm inside a snow globe, all safe and perfect."

We just lay there, not saying anything for a while. It was easy to be quiet together when we weren't even looking at each other. I could hear him breathing—his lips made little puffing sounds with each intake of air, like he was really thinking about each breath and celebrating it with a tiny puff. I'm sure it wasn't intentional, but it was all I could think about as we lay there. That and the fact that his hair was stretching out to touch mine, interlocking with a piece of me.

I could feel him, too—the weight of his body on the other side of the couch made me feel like I was lying at a downhill angle, my head slightly lower than my body. I closed my eyes and breathed in, trying to smell him—that delicious smell of cinnamon and soap I'd breathed in at Matt's the other night. But all I could smell at the moment was microwave oatmeal, the Maple Brown Sugar kind.

"What's the story with the guy your parents are trying to set you up with?" he asked, breaking the silence and bringing thoughts of Hunter into the room.

"No story."

"I'm intrigued. There must be a story—your mom was working so hard. He's not a cousin, is he?"

"No!"

"It's a small town. It's important to check."

"He's a friend of the family. His mom and my mom are church ladies together."

"I see," he murmured.

"He's not my type."

"What is your type?" I could hear the smile, could feel his body shift on the couch when he asked that. He was teasing me again—flirting en route to his self-inflicted dead end.

"I'm not sure," I answered honestly. I considered my afternoon with Hunter, how it had left me with more questions than answers. There wasn't a lot of risk in filtering my comments with this guy—nothing to lose, right? We (well, he) had already established that there was nowhere for us to go in the romance department, so it wasn't like I could ruin anything. "I just know that what I'm looking for doesn't exist in Milton."

Sebastian put his hand up on the window, tracing the outline of a tree in the yard with his finger. "What are you going to do when you graduate?"

"That's the question of the season, isn't it?"

"What do people from Milton do, generally speaking?" I could hear a little judgment in his voice, and it was interesting to feel myself put a little shield up to defend my town.

I was allowed to make fun of Milton, but outsiders were not. "What do you think? We raise cows, start a dairy, and inbreed."

That got him laughing. "That's what I thought. The Midwest is weird."

"Yep." The sarcasm started to take over, and I let it. "Actually, something you should know about me is that I only have three toes. It's a genetic deformity passed down through generations. It's because we don't leave our small town, so everyone mates within our own family, and things have really devolved in the past few generations."

"Okay, point taken." He adjusted on the couch, and his head came closer to mine. I didn't move an inch, hoping it would slowly creep toward me through the course of the afternoon until we would be lying there, cheek to cheek, at some point in the very near future. "Seriously, though, what are you going to do after you graduate? Do you stick around here? College?"

"I don't know." He didn't know me, so he didn't know the expectations that had been set for me here in Milton. He didn't know that I was at the top of our class. He didn't know I was supposed to be one of the Milton residents that went off and did great things that the local newsletter would write about. He didn't know I couldn't figure out what I wanted to do with my life, other than start it somewhere that wasn't here. He didn't know how much it scared me that I didn't have all the answers about my life's plans. "I haven't figured it out yet."

"Fair enough." And that was it. No comment, no announcement about missing deadlines or application dates, no question about what I *would* do with my time. "You have your whole life to figure it out, right? Why force it now?"

"Precisely." I smiled, quietly celebrating the fact that I'd just said, out loud for the first time, that I was maybe, possibly, not going to college next year. "I just know I want to get out of Milton. I don't really belong here—I even hate venison. What Northern Minnesotan doesn't like fresh deer meat?"

"You do belong here, though." He paused for only a moment, then clarified. "The three toes—they need to stay local, I think. Don't bring your inbreeding out into the rest of the country. A fourth or—God forbid—a fifth might grow back if you mate outside your family."

"Right. Inner-circle mating is of the utmost importance when you want to carry on a distinguished trait like three toes."

"Exactly."

As we lay there, bantering and goofing off and making each other laugh, I couldn't stop thinking about one thing in the back of my mind. *Why can't he be interested in me?* If he were even remotely attracted to me, wouldn't he be going after something? Isn't that what guys do? Was it wrong that that was what I wanted to do?

"What are *you* going to do after high school?" I asked, rather than bringing up the question I wanted to bring up, which was, *Why don't you want to kiss me?*

He laughed a little, then said, "I hope there is an 'after high school.'"

"Ooh, aren't you cryptic?" I teased. He was totally playing the bad-boy card. *As if.* "What's that supposed to mean?"

"Things are a little, uh, weird back home. Plans change, stuff shifts, you know."

"Such as?"

He chuckled again, and he stretched his hands up over his head. When he did, they touched my shoulders, and I shuddered. I wanted it to not be an accident, but I knew it was. He pulled them back against his sides as quickly as they'd come, as though they'd never been near me in the first place. "Some things happened before Christmas break that . . . complicated things. I got a little messed up in some stuff." He rearranged himself on the couch, and suddenly his legs were draped up over the back of the sofa, his body lying right next to my head.

"Like, drug stuff?"

"No, nothing like that."

"Illegal stuff?"

"Just stuff."

I got it. He didn't want to talk about it—he didn't seem like a depressed kind of guy, and he clearly wasn't an alcoholic (I worked at a bar, and he'd never once tried to seduce me just so I'd serve him a shot of tequila). Not drugs. What was his deal? "So these 'things'—they affected your plans for next year?"

"Not really—I don't know if I really had any plans, now that I've had the time to think about it. I guess I'm just taking winter break to start to figure me out after screwing up, you know? If you ask my parents, who have their own version of my story, I'm sort of fucking myself over for next year by questioning a bunch of stuff, which is getting me nowhere." I tilted my head back to get a look at him, and saw that his eyes were closed.

"I'm sort of doing the same thing." I sighed, closing my own eyes. He relaxed me. It felt like I could trust him, even though everything he was telling me should have made me worried about what his issues were. I had my own issues—did I have room for his? "I'm sort of fucking up my plans for next year by thinking about a bunch of stuff too—I mean, college has always been a sure thing, but I don't feel like it's the right choice for me right now. I don't know what I want, but I do know I don't want to waste a bunch of money to sit around watching soap operas with a bunch of faux intellectuals."

"Soap operas?" He laughed. "What kind of colleges were you applying to? Last I heard, college was about literary analysis and gender studies and poetry slams. Much more Hemingway than *The Hills*."

"I don't know." I was laughing too. "My image of college involves dorm parties and sleepovers and drunk frat boys. You can see why it's not that tempting." I shifted on the couch so that I, too, had my legs up over the back of the couch. I was lying next to him now, both our heads hanging upside down over the front of the couch, looking out the window behind us. Our arms were stretched out next to each other, two inches separating us.

He twisted his head to look at me and smiled. "We're the experts at screwing our own lives up, aren't we?"

"I wouldn't have it any other way," I agreed. I got the impression I wasn't going to get anything more out of him about the "things" that had messed him up, so I just lay there quietly, soaking in his closeness. To me it was a highly charged silence—the whole time I felt like I was shooting off *fuck me* beams and he was defending against them with his secret male-power armor.

I wanted to touch him, wanted to just reach out a finger to show him I was interested. But he'd made it clear—it wasn't going to happen. I refused to be desperate; I refused to act like *that* girl. After a few minutes I started to imagine things. Felt his hand moving—but it never brushed against me. Then I sensed his body shifting closer—but when I looked, he was as still as glass.

Just when I thought I could feel his thigh pressing against mine as it draped over the back of the couch, my phone rang. I would never know if what I thought I felt was there, because I answered the call. Was it a phantom touch, an imagined closeness, or something real?

"Come over now," Sadie whispered, her voice shaking on the other side of the line.

"I'm on my way." I glanced at Sebastian, whose eyes were closed again. His leg was back on his side of the sofa, nowhere near mine. "Is everything okay?" I asked her, though I knew it wasn't.

Sadie drew a ragged breath. "I'm pretty sure I'm pregnant."

**12. "THIS IS NOT THE WAY I PLANNED**
my life, Chaz." Sadie met me at the front door, holding a plastic pregnancy test stick. A tiny drop of pee was visible inside the clear plastic cap. That was the only thing I could see when I looked at it—I didn't want to see the little plus sign, so I just focused on that captured droplet of pee when Sadie waved the thing in front of my face. "I can't have a baby."

"Okay, Sade, let's just think, okay?"

"I need to get it out of me!" Sadie looked terrified. At the sound of her own voice saying those words, she broke into a mess of tears. "I can't do that, though, Chaz. I can't!"

"You have options—um, okay, let's sit down?"

"Why?" Sadie demanded. "Why did this happen?"

I measured my words carefully, then realized I just had to hit her with it. "Did you use a condom?"

"Of course we did!"

"Every time?"

"Yes! I mean, we did when it mattered."

"What do you mean, 'when it mattered'?" I was trying not to sound judgmental.

Sadie sat on the couch and pulled her knees up to hide her face against them. "I'm his first, and he's mine—so we just made sure we always put one on eventually."

"Eventually?"

"I mean, I know he doesn't have any diseases or anything, so there were a few times when I let him, um . . ." Sadie peeked up at me. "Um, start a little before he put the condom on." She threw her head back down, embarrassed.

"Okay," I said levelly. It was too late for lessons. I couldn't really say, *Yeah, that's the definition of unprotected sex. Even if he didn't finish inside, a little bit can sneak out ahead of time.* I didn't say that. My job was to comfort, not to question. What I did say was, "Okay, so that means we have to figure out what you're going to do. Maybe you should take another test, just to be sure?" My voice was übercalm and adeptly hid the internal bubbling and rumbling. Why the fuck was the universe messing with Sadie's crystal-clear future rather than my murky one?

"I got one of the three-packs from the gas station."

"Was your aunt working?"

"Yeah," Sadie flushed. "I stole it."

I nodded. Considering the circumstances, that was probably a good call. In a place like Milton, pregnancy test purchases by teens would make the front page of the town newsletter. "Have you used all the tests?"

"Yes."

"Positive every time?"

"Yes."

"Okay." I grabbed her hand. "Have you told Trav?"

"No."

"Are you going to?"

"I don't know."

"Do you want something to eat?"

"What?" Sadie looked confused.

"Are you hungry? Your body is working hard. You must be hungry."

"What are you, my mom? Since when do you get nervous energy out with cooking?"

I laughed. "Since my best friend found out she was pregnant."

"Oh, gosh, Chaz. Don't say it out loud again."

"If we ignore the facts, the facts won't change. So we might as well face reality and start to deal with it, yes?" I heard myself saying this, but I didn't feel the way I sounded. I was flat-out scared for her.

"Can't I just curl up in bed and hide away for, like, nine months until this all goes away?"

"And then what?" I asked gently. "Then you have a baby?"

"I don't know!" Sadie screamed, freaking out again. She was shaking and rocking, and her hand felt sweaty tucked inside mine. "I don't know if I can do that."

I let her calm down before I asked, "Would you consider an abortion?"

Her voice was clear when she said, "I feel like it's my only choice."

"That's not the best way to make that decision—by eliminating other choices without thinking through everything." I didn't want Sadie to make this decision with fear staring her down. We had to talk about this rationally so she could figure out what she really wanted. What she could handle.

"I'm seventeen, Chaz." Her blue eyes glowed beneath a film of tears. "Not twenty-five. I don't want a baby. I can't have a baby."

"What about adoption?" I suggested.

"What do you have against abortion? It's the easiest way—over and done."

Deep down I guess I agreed. But I knew she was just acting tough—this wasn't Sadie talking. It was someone scared and freaked out who wasn't thinking things through. "I will support whatever choice you make, Sadie. I just want to make sure you think about it. I don't want you to regret anything."

"Do I have to tell Trav?"

"Not if you don't want to."

"Good." Tears were flowing down Sadie's cheeks now, leaving wet streaks on her flushed face. "I wouldn't know what to say."

I sighed. "I think you'll feel better if you talk to him about it. You got into this together—it might help to talk to him, tell him what you're thinking. It's not like he's just some guy. It's Trav."

"I don't know." Sadie buried her head in my lap, and I stroked her hair. She was like a cat—a sweet, tiny little kitty-cat, but this one had a baby in her belly. "Will you stay over?"

"Of course." As soon as I said that, I realized I hadn't yet seen my parents since they'd gotten home from Minneapolis. I was avoiding that situation to deal with this one—when had my life gone all to hell? Why were my options for the evening cancer or teen pregnancy?

The main objective of the night was avoiding Sadie's parents. Sadie knew she couldn't even look at them if she was going to keep herself together, so we put in a movie and holed up in her room. Neither of us watched it—it was some stupid romantic comedy with a ridiculous kissing climax—but as soon as it was over, we threw another one in the DVD player and pretended to be engrossed every time her mom came by.

Sadie fell asleep, slumped against me, sometime around midnight. Her parents were in bed, and she was knocked out (and knocked up), but I was spinning. It felt as if the planets were conspiring against me, trying to cut me apart piece by piece.

Breaking things down, this is where things stood that night:

First, my best friend was in the family way, as they say, and I couldn't help her.

Second, my family was a mess. I criticized my mom for being emotionally constipated and complained about them keeping things from me—yet I couldn't look my dad in the eye and had spent an entire day going out of my way to avoid them rather than talking to them about stuff that was ripping our family in pieces. Was I becoming—horror of horrors—someone like my mom?

And finally, I was obsessed with a boy who didn't want

me and was messing with the one who did . . . which equals fucked-up bitch, when you think about it that way.

I knew I couldn't do anything about any one of those things. But that night, sitting there supporting the weight of my best friend's sleeping body, I just wanted to fix Sadie. As the tears rolled down my cheeks and I sobbed—keeping as still as possible so as not to wake my best friend—all I could think was: *This should totally be me. I'm the one who deserves this mess.* Sadie was an angel, with a future perfectly mapped. Fate had messed this one up.

Fate really should be fucking with me.

The next morning I woke up sore and unrested. I'd slept most of the night half sitting up, with Sadie passed out against me. My mind didn't feel much better than it had the night before either—there was so much crap filling my head that it felt like I had to do an emotional purge somehow to get it all out of me. Trouble was, I didn't have anyone to talk to, even if I'd wanted to. Everyone had their own problems to deal with.

When Sadie stirred next to me, I watched her pretty face wake up to the day. At first she looked so calm and sweet and at peace. I knew the instant the memory of yesterday came crashing back into her, since her face filled with sorrow and fear. She looked at me watching her and started to cry again. I hugged her to me, and we lay like that for a long time, each of us thinking silently about what was going to happen.

"Will you drive me to Flanders today?" Sadie asked, breaking the silence.

"Are you sure?" I pressed. Flanders had a free clinic where they did abortions. Everyone in Milton knew about it, and people often drove by, laughing at the handful of protestors and making fun of people who got themselves in bad situations. We were those people now. "I'll take you if you want to go."

"I'm ready." Sadie's mouth was set in a determined line. "I'm going to get an abortion."

I nodded to show my support. "Okay." I had always been pro-choice, even though we had learned a different way of thinking during our confirmation class at church. As soon as I was old enough to understand my body and pay attention to the fact that I knew what was best for me, generally speaking, I felt pretty strongly about a person's right to make their own choice about their body. I never got into discussions about it with anyone else—it wasn't worth my breath to argue with people in this town—but Sadie had always known where I stood.

But the fact that I am pro-choice does not automatically mean I'm pro-abortion. I'd never really thought about abortion and what it really meant in such a personal, direct way. I hadn't thought I'd ever have to be a part of a decision that would end with a choice to do something like this. So I knew how I felt in theory—but now, faced with this cold, hard reality, I was scared out of my mind. I thought I knew what was probably best for Sadie, but how could I figure out if it really *was* the right decision? And this wasn't even my choice. If it had been, I didn't know what I would have done.

We got dressed quickly, neither of us bothering to shower. Sadie was completely silent while she pulled on a pair of running pants and an old sweatshirt with a hood. I put on my jeans but borrowed a clean shirt. Her parents were gone when we went out to the kitchen, so we grabbed granola bars from the cupboard and hit the road.

Sadie cried quietly the whole way to Flanders. I didn't know what to say, so I just kept my eyes on the road. "You know you don't have to do this today," I said when we were halfway there. "We can just talk to the doctor, hear more about what your choices are." She ignored me and stared out her window.

When we pulled up to the clinic, there was one lame picketer in snow pants and a parka, sitting on a chair, holding a sign with a picture of a baby bundled in a blue blanket. We parked on the street, not in the clinic lot, and I turned off the engine. Sadie looked at me, and it took every ounce of emotional power to hold back the tears I so desperately needed to shed. I didn't know why, but I didn't want to cry. I didn't want to see Sadie see me break down. I had to be strong for her.

"I always thought I would be a young mom." She was crying again. "Trav and I have actually talked about it—after college, when we were both back in Milton together, we'd get married and start our family. That's the hardest part."

I just sat there, looking at her, with a rock holding my stomach down, keeping it from fluttering away with nerves as we sat outside the clinic.

Sadie continued, "If he knew what I'm about to do, that would be the end for us." She stopped crying, and her face was blank, staring at me without seeing me—the way I sometimes did when my mom was lecturing me about something meaningless. You try to fix your eyes on a target, but they refuse to cooperate and just stare blankly into space without focusing. "I know he wouldn't want me to do this."

I took a breath, then said, "It's not too late to talk to him first."

She finally focused in on me. I could see her eyes change, watched her mouth set into a firm line. "It's Christmas, Chaz. I feel like God is watching me more than ever right now. How can I do this at Christmas?"

I knew the question was rhetorical, and I decided not to answer. She had to make her own decision and come to it in her own time. Whatever I said was just going to complicate this further for her.

After a few minutes of sitting there without moving—the whole time the picketer was watching our car carefully, waiting to see if he needed to make a move with his bundle-of-joy poster—Sadie leaned over and turned the keys in the ignition. "Just drive," she said.

So that's what I did. We drove back to Milton and went past her house. Her mom's car was in the driveway, so I decided to keep driving. We pulled up at Matt's, and I led Sadie inside, back to a booth in the far back corner where I knew no one would bug us. I went up to the counter and filled a couple of glasses with root beer. Neither of us touched the soda, but it gave us something to do while we sat there. I watched the bubbles float up to the surface and pop, hundreds of little bubbles floating and popping and fizzing.

If our life were a movie and I were running the voice-over narration, I would say those bubbles were like dreams, I guess. Getting pushed around by a higher force (my straw, in this case) and hitting something that made them pop. Dreams that fizzle out into a whole lot of nothing. Or dreams that were never anything in the first place.

"I need a week," Sadie said, breaking the hour-long silence we had going. "I need to get past Christmas. I need to tell Trav."

I nodded. I knew she didn't need my approval, but I felt like I should give her some sign I agreed with her decision. I didn't know what I felt, but I knew I'd support my best friend, however she decided to deal with it. "Okay," was all I said.

"Will you bring me to Trav's now?" Sadie had already stood up and was on her way out the door. The arch of her back, the way she carried herself, had changed. Not because she was pregnant—that would be ridiculous; she was probably only a month or two along—but because it seemed like the weight of the world was on her shoulders. Things had changed.

"Yeah," I told Sadie as she walked away. Then, more to myself, I said, "I can do that."

# 13.

"I THOUGHT WE COULD HAVE DINNER
together." My mom whined this, sounding like a little kid.
"We have things to discuss."

"I can't." I hustled past her toward a much-needed
shower. I had dropped Sadie off at Trav's, then driven home
to change into my running clothes. It was cold outside, but
I had needed a run to clear my head. Now I was back and
had less than an hour to make myself human again before it
was back to Matt's for another night of the same old same
old. "I'm sorry."

My mom pinched her lips à la Miriam Johnson. "No, I'm sorry. I wish we had time to sit down as a family."

"Yeah, we seem to be missing that whole family connection thing lately, don't we?" I felt bad after saying that, but I was reeling from my day, and it still stung whenever I thought about my parents' lies and secrets. I continued up the stairs.

My mom yelled after me, "You better be here for Christmas Eve with the Johnsons!"

"I wouldn't miss it," I muttered.

Once in the shower I turned everything inside myself off. The steam billowed around me, filling every pore with a misty thickness. It felt like my body was swelling with the bullshit stuffed inside me, which had nowhere to go. The steam was sealing it all in. I twisted the shower handle to cold, trying to rinse the steam away. It was stifling me, making me choke in the haze.

I turned the water off and stepped out, toweling off before wiping down the mirror. I looked at myself and turned to the side, pushing my abdomen out. My hip bones stuck out too far, and my tits were mini, but the tiny little belly I had going when I pushed it out like this made me look a little preggers. I relaxed, and my stomach fell flat again. Sadie's wouldn't do that. Hers would just keep getting bigger.

Back in my room I was disgusted to find that my Matt's

T-shirts were all dirty. Laundry had become my own responsibility about two years ago, and I was bad at it. I grabbed the shirt closest to the top of my dirty clothes pile and gave it a deep sniff. Not terrible—a few hours at Matt's and I'd just smell like fresh grease anyway. It could be worse.

When I got downstairs, my dad was sitting on the couch in the living room waiting for me. He had a magazine open, but it was on a spread advertising Mint Milano cookies, so I knew he wasn't really reading it. "Hi, Dad."

"Hey, pumpkin." He smiled at me reassuringly, which made me a little uncomfortable. "What have you been up to all day?"

"Not much." I grabbed my shoes from the basket by the front door and started untying the laces. "How'd it go on Monday?" My mom was in the kitchen, talking on the phone, so I knew I had a few minutes alone with my dad.

"Good, good."

"What's the story, then?" I had my laces untied and was starting to fasten the shoes onto my feet. It was weird how my voice defied my feelings—I sounded way more cool and controlled than I'd thought I would, considering the fact that I was freaking out about what he'd learned from the doctor. I guess my morning had numbed me so I could handle challenging conversations. "Everything good?"

"They did some tests and talked about some options." His voice was even, and I knew he was trying to sound casual. "We should know more in a few days."

"Okay."

"Chastity?" He was waiting for me to look up. I did. "I'm sorry we kept it from you."

"It's fine." I smiled, attempting to show how little I cared. I was fooling no one. "I have to get to work."

He stood up. "Got a hug for your old dad?"

I made it a quick squeeze, feeling his chubby belly smush under mine. "See you later, old man." Dad grinned, and I felt a little bit better.

You would think after our afternoon together I would have heard from Sebastian, right? I mean, we had sort of clicked, I thought. Sure, he wasn't going to be the sex toy I'd hoped he would be, but we could still be friends. I liked his attitude, and I guess I thought—if nothing else—he was sort of entertained by me. He was an escape from Milton, and I had started to think maybe there was hope for a little something . . . a friendship, even.

But no. During the course of a shift at Matt's—one whole dinner rush and the usual Christmas week evening crowd— he didn't make a single appearance. He hadn't called my cell, nothing. Not even a text to make sure I was cool after yester-day's sudden departure. He made me want to scream. I had never doubted myself like this before, and it killed me that he had this kind of power over me. How could I have been so stupid to let my guard down around him?

I vowed to take the control back again, this time for good, and stop letting a silly little crush mess with my head the way it was. Enough was enough. "Hey, Danny," I called out during my break. I was sitting at the bar drinking a Coke. Danny was washing dishes behind the bar and immediately sauntered over.

"Yes, your highness?" I was pretty sure he was wearing a tinted lip color. His lips were unnaturally rich-looking. "You called?"

"What are you up to after work?"

"Hanging out with you."

Danny was a little cheesy, but his arrogance cracked me up. "Okay," I agreed. "You guys want to come over to my house again?" I knew my parents would be fine with it—my mom would probably make us snacks to get back on my good side.

Danny narrowed his eyes. "Can we make it a smaller group this time?" He leaned in toward me. Now I was sure his lips were tinted with something. They couldn't possibly be that soft and supple-looking without enhancement. "Skip the little girls we had over last time—maybe just you, me, Ange, and Ryan?"

"Yeah," I shrugged. "You don't want to bring your fan club along? You're sure?"

"I don't need fans—I'll have you." He was totally serious. For real. Danny Idol had just uttered one of the lamest lines in the history of lines, and he had no idea it hadn't had the effect he'd hoped it would.

"Danny," I said, grabbing his shirt and pulling him in closer to me across the bar. "This could be fun tonight. But if you say anything that ridiculous again, I guarantee this will be the lamest night you've had since you became Danny Idol."

He seemed to get it, since he lifted his hands up in a surrender pose and backed up. When he was back in place in front of the sink, scrubbing glasses, he looked over at me and winked. The rest of the night Danny was on his best behavior, cracking cute little jokes every time I passed him on my way to the kitchen or beaming at me from across the room. He was pretty charming, and I could understand his appeal for just about every girl (and grown woman) in town.

Almost as soon as we got to my house, we left Angela and Ryan in the basement and went upstairs to my room. My parents' room was way down the hall, so I wasn't too concerned about privacy. It was also after midnight, so they'd been asleep for at least two hours.

"What's this?" Danny asked, standing near my bed and pointing to a picture of me at a track meet back in eighth grade. "Cute hair."

"Funny," I stated. "Feel free to look around. Poke through all my personal stuff."

"Thanks, I think I will." His eyes were a little red around the edges, and I was pretty sure he'd smoked up out back of Matt's before we'd left for my house. He was handling himself pretty well, considering, but it still irked me a little bit that he felt the need to get high before hanging out.

"Let me know if you have any questions." I said. "I'd be happy to walk you through the embarrassing stages of my life, one by one."

He chuckled, fingering one of my EVERYONE'S A WINNER track ribbons from elementary school. I sat at my desk chair and watched him browsing around my room. He asked me some questions about Sadie and my parents—the subjects of most of my pictures—and we talked about a few of his favorite bands.

The conversation was very forgettable, but I was enjoying myself. Danny had a laid-back quality that amused me, and he was an easy conversationalist.

"Do you ever just chill?" he asked suddenly, watching me watch him from across the room. "I feel like you're studying me like some kind of animal."

"Maybe I am." I shrugged and lifted one eyebrow.

"You're sexy, Chaz." His cocky, know-it-all smile was back. Maybe this was his flirt face? "You know that, though, don't you?" He stopped his wandering and sat down on my bed. He patted the space next to him, so I climbed in and wondered where this might be going. No one would deny that Danny Idol was eye candy, and he certainly wasn't a boring option. What harm could come from a little playful flirting and maybe some making out?

He started to tickle me—was this his way of breaking down my guard?

There are three girls at school (yes, Tina Zander is one of them) who are widely known as sluts. In truth they haven't slept with many people—or maybe even anyone. But they are very indiscriminating about who they'll make out with and who is allowed to put hands down their pants. They "get around," to use the common language.

And that is the difference between them and me—I'm picky, and I'm not interested in getting a reputation. Sure, I want experience. But I've always been careful about who I experiment with.

So when faced with the opportunity to exercise my sexuality with Danny Idol, the hometown hero who was only around for the holidays . . . well, it was a pretty easy decision. He was cute, made me laugh, and wouldn't have the opportunity to talk about our rendezvous in the high school locker room after hockey practice.

He tickled me again, this time reaching for my hips. I squirmed and let him run his fingers over me some more. My body moved toward him as he reached around to tickle my back. I pushed my hips against him, and that was all he needed as a green light.

Suddenly, his lips were on me, kissing me on the mouth, on the ear, down my neck. His hands moved fast, and he had unsnapped my bra without me even knowing. I was impressed. The guy had moves, and I told him so. That made him laugh, and he wrapped his hand around my leg to pull it up and around him. He was on top of me, pushing down hard. I was short of breath and really starting to get into it. I could get used to this—unlike Hunter, who left me feeling about as charged as a dead battery, Danny had a power that made me want to grab his hair and pull. He had me fired up.

When his hand moved to flip open the button on my jeans, I let him. He pulled my pants down, and I was lying there in just my underwear with my Matt's T-shirt twisted around my chest. Momentarily, I thought about how much action this T-shirt had seen lately. My lucky tee.

"You're so hot," he breathed in my ear. I shut my eyes, and my mind flashed to Sebastian. I let my imagination take me where it wanted, and I pictured Sebastian lying here on top of me, muttering the same nonsense in my ear. When I thought about Sebastian, and the way I felt when I was with him, it made me tingle. I got totally into it, and Danny and I made out for I don't know how long.

Things sort of stayed on a plateau, until suddenly I felt his hand slip down my side and tug at the top of my underwear. Simultaneously, he was pulling his own pants down, bringing his body and mine even closer together. I wanted this and was ready to go for it—this was it.

Danny breathed in my ear. Things kept going, further and further, and within minutes Danny's pants were down around his knees and he was coming at me. I felt naked skin against my leg; then he brought his mouth to my ear. He whispered, "I swear I'm clean, so we don't need protection."

"Nuh-uh," I murmured back. "I won't do that."

"I'm allergic to latex," he whispered then. "I can't wear a condom—let's just try? For a couple seconds?"

It wasn't just the image of Sadie that stopped me then. It was Sadie and Sebastian and even a little bit of Hunter. But it was also the begging, together with the expectation that I'd be stupid enough to have sex with him without protection. I wasn't a fool. He was a wannabe rock star who used the lingering fumes of his almost-fame to get whatever he could. I was sure he'd been with at least a few girls since his *Idol* days. *Ick.* If I slept with him without protection, it was like I was sleeping with everyone else he'd slept with. "You're on your own," I said, then slipped off the bed and pulled my underwear back up.

I walked over to my desk and sat down. Danny lay on my bed and finished himself off into a tissue while I checked my e-mail.

Why and how had this ever seemed like a reasonable idea?

 **"I WAS THINKING WE SHOULD MAKE**
a stop in the admissions office next time your father and I are
down at the U." My mom was driving me to Sadie's the next
morning before my shift at Matt's and delivered this message
via the rearview mirror. She looked at me sitting in the backseat
and lifted her brows. "What do you think?"

"I think they'll appreciate that," I replied, staring out
the window. As if the admissions office at the University of
Minnesota was going to talk to my mom, one of fifty thousand
parents of applicants.

"I don't understand why you haven't heard anything, Chastity. I heard several of the women at church talking about their children going to the U next year, and I just can't figure out why they've all heard and you haven't." My mom was gripping the wheel tightly, her knuckles taking the brunt of her stress. "You are the star of your class, and your application was in very early, from what I can tell."

"It's a mystery."

My mom thudded her palm against the steering wheel. I was frustrating her. "I worry about you." This is what she'd been getting to—we weren't having a relaxed conversation about the college admissions process and waiting for acceptances to arrive. She was just taking the long road to a nice, hefty discussion about my future. "What are your plans?" she demanded.

Gosh, I thought. *It's so tempting to tell you my fears and dreams when you threaten me like that, Mom.* Out loud I said, "Dunno. Maybe I'll get rejected at the U and work at Matt's forever."

"Don't be cute." She didn't mean "cute." She meant "feisty." She was mad because I was being feisty. "For one, you're not going to get rejected at the U—don't even talk like that. Your life would be ruined if that were true." She narrowed her eyes at me, and I looked away—this was the reason I didn't like to talk to her. She was full of judgment and criticism and opinions about where I should go in life. "And I know you too well, Chastity Bryan—I know you have no plans to work at Matt's forever."

"Too true," I agreed.

"Don't you get it?" she shrieked. "You need to think about your future if you want to have the best things in life." The conversation had moved to the point of hysterics. I couldn't figure out why she was suddenly so worked up about this, and then she said this (which led to the next thing): "You're overlooking a great opportunity, Chaz."

"I sent in my application," I lied. We were only a few blocks away from Sadie's then, so I didn't have to put up with much more of this. As if I needed her stress on top of all my own. "What else am I supposed to do?"

She blew a thin sliver of air out from between her lips. "I'm not talking about college, Chastity. I'm talking about Hunter Johnson."

"What?" She was crazy. Where had this come from?

"I know you've been spending time together—Miriam has kept me clued in. But I don't feel like you're taking it seriously enough." She smiled at me chummily, as though we were best buds, confidants. "You haven't even bought him a Christmas present, have you?"

Finally, we arrived at Sadie's, and I had an escape route out of the conversation—I hopped out of the car. Sadie was peeking out the window, watching me walk up the front path. "See you later, Mom."

"Do you want me to pick something up for Hunter?" she called after me, out her window. "Remember we're all going to be together for Christmas Eve. We got a call from your father's doctor today—it looks like the cancer hasn't spread, so it's cause for celebration!"

She'd made my dad a side note again, an afterthought, as though I hadn't been waiting desperately to hear what was going on.

"Maybe I could buy Hunter a nice sweater for you?"

I looked back at her and saw she was wearing a smile that freakishly resembled Miriam Johnson's—my two moms. "That would be great," I said. "I think a sweater would be the perfect gift for me to give Hunter to show him *just* how I feel."

When I walked into Sadie's house, the first thing I noticed was that she was wearing the same outfit she'd been wearing the morning before. She looked like she'd just rolled out of bed, and I wondered if she'd been at Trav's until late last night, talking about the pregnancy.

Sadie held her finger up to her lips and hustled me through

the living room and the kitchen, into her bedroom. Her parents were upstairs—I could hear them singing Christmas carols. How festive.

"How did it go?" I pressed, as soon as we were safely in Sadie's room. "Are you okay?"

Sadie stared at me with this wild-eyed, sort of manic expression. It was obvious she hadn't slept more than an hour or two since I'd last seen her. "I didn't tell him. I haven't told anyone."

"What happened? How could you keep it from him?" I blurted this before I could think about what I was saying, and as soon as it was out, Sadie started to cry.

They weren't the same vulnerable, scared tears they had been the day before—she just seemed angry and tired and bitter. "God, Chaz, I already feel like shit, and I'm a liar, and I don't need you accusing me of hiding things. You, of all people." *Ouch.* "Just give me some time, okay?" She said this aggressively, not in her usual Sadie voice. There wasn't a hint of patience in her tone, and I knew she was ripped apart and on edge and just needed me to be a friend.

I nodded, uncertain of what more I could say. Sadie and I had always been great about telling each other things (at least Sadie had always told me everything), but now it felt like there was a mile-wide divide between us. Despite the fact that I was freaked out about the baby and about my dad and about every other uncertain part of my life and Sadie's, I had to keep up a certain level of confidence to get us both through. I knew she didn't want to see my shell crack—she just needed me to be the strong, confident (and never-scared) Chaz that I was so good at playing. "You can have all the time you need. What do you want me to do? What can I help with?"

"Nothing," she spat out venomously. Then she sighed. "I'm not pissed at you." She said this with an edge to her voice, but I knew she was telling the truth. At least Sadie felt comfortable expressing herself around me; she knew she could be however horrible to me she wanted to be, and I'd still love her. "After you dropped me off outside Trav's yesterday, I panicked and walked home. I couldn't be with him last night."

I stroked her hair while she lay on her soft flower pillow, and told her, "You should have called me. I would have picked you up."

"I know." She nodded. "I'm just so embarrassed. You have your life so together, and you always know what to do about everything, and I'm such a mess, and you don't need to be around me right now."

"Oh, Sadie, that's not true." I pulled her against me, holding her head in my lap so I didn't have to look at her while I hid from the truth. "I'm here, aren't I? That's by choice." If I hadn't been such a chickenshit, I would have told her why she was wrong about everything she'd just said.

I would have told her that the future scared me more than anything, despite my external confidence about everything. I would have shared my doubts about college for next year. I would have told her that I had no idea what I was going to do with my life, and that I was afraid that meant I'd be stuck in this town forever. I would have admitted that I was scared for her, I was scared for me, and I was scared about my family. I would have confessed that I was frightened to be with her at that very moment, and that I was terrified about being expected to know what to do when my best friend got pregnant.

But I didn't tell her any of that. I just reassured her that everything would work out and that she could handle anything and that I would be there for her. The same bullshit that I knew would work to make her feel better and make me feel like even more of a liar.

"I wish I had all the answers," Sadie said, nestling against me even closer.

So do I, I thought.

"You are a naughty girl," Angela called out as soon as I walked in the front door of Matt's a little while later. Sadie had sent me away, promising to nap before her eve of Christmas Eve celebration with Trav that night. "Tsk-tsk."

I blushed. What had Danny told them on the drive home last night? I chose the silent path and didn't respond. Angela would come out with it soon. "Good morning," I said instead. I was working the lunch shift today—in at eleven, out around three. This was my last shift before Christmas, my last easy out of family life before the holidays officially descended.

"What happened last night?" She said eagerly. "Did you guys do it?"

"No."

She giggled. "No? I don't believe you."

"You should." I grabbed my apron and tied it around my waist. "He jacked off while I checked my e-mail."

Angela laughed hysterically. "That's classic. You are such a bad liar."

"It's the truth."

"Whatever. I'll get the real story from Danny." Ange was starting to look annoyed. But I wouldn't make up a story that good—she had to know that.

"Okay. But that's what happened."

That was the last of our conversation for a while. Matt had us filling ketchup bottles (his cost-saving trick was using this giant, industrial-size generic ketchup to fill Heinz bottles) and saltshakers and wiping down tables. By the time we'd done our chores, the lunch rush had started to file in, and there wasn't much time for chatting anyway. I knew Danny was on the schedule for noon, so I expected him to come in any minute and inspire Angela's inquisition to start back up.

Just before noon, as I was coming out from the kitchen with an armload of orders, I spotted Sebastian at the front door, looking at his usual table—which was full. My whole body responded when I saw him standing there. I was full of electricity and excitement and giddiness. I smiled at him, dropped the food off at its rightful table, and went over to say hi.

"Hey." He pulled off his winter hat.

"Want to sit at the bar today?" I suggested. I didn't want him to leave.

"Yeah," he nodded slowly. "Okay. Change is good, right?"

Sometimes, I thought. *And sometimes it sucks.* I went around the back of the bar to get him something to drink, and he settled in on the same bar stool Hunter had sat on two days earlier. "How have you been?" I asked.

"Decent. How's your friend? Everything okay?" He was asking about Sadie—it felt like a lifetime had passed since I'd last seen him. So much had happened since then.

"It's complicated."

"Gotcha." I knew he was watching me while I wiped down the counter behind the bar. "Anything you want to talk about?"

For some reason that simple offer meant more to me than he could have imagined. It felt like such a regular thing to say—I mean, that's what you're supposed to say when it seems like something is going on with someone, right?—but it was the tone of his voice that made me know he meant it. He really was willing to listen to me, and I knew already that he wouldn't judge or jump to conclusions or freak me out about stuff.

But it was personal—I couldn't go there with a stranger. I couldn't tell him Sadie's secret, no matter how much it was eating me up inside. "No," I said finally. "Thanks, though." I smiled to show him I was strong and not sinking into a mess of emotional quicksand.

"Maybe we could go somewhere later?" he suggested, apparently seeing through my thin veil of strength. "Just talk?"

Just talk. Of course. "Yeah. That'd be great."

"Now get back to work," he commanded. "I need to order my lunch."

I did as I was told, and he sat there watching me go about my work, periodically reading the same book he'd been toting around all week. When Danny showed up for his shift—an hour late—I didn't really pay attention to him. Until I saw him and Angela talking together, right behind the bar, just steps away from Sebastian.

I dropped the burgers I was carrying at table six and hustled back to intercept their conversation. But I was too late—I heard Danny saying, "It was a *great* night—Chaz is a sweet treat." *Ack.* They'd been talking about me—right there, right in front of Sebastian.

Sebastian was blatantly staring at them, openly listening to their conversation. Angela noticed him sitting there at the bar then, and her hand flew up to cover her mouth. She looked at me desperately and mouthed, *I'm sorry.* But it was too late. Clearly, Sebastian had heard their whole discussion about how I'd gotten it on with Danny the night before. I could tell from Angela's horrified reaction that they'd gone into a squirm-worthy level of detail.

I just shrugged to show her I didn't really care—I certainly didn't feel guilty about what I'd done with Danny, and I couldn't be embarrassed about it if it had been my choice to get it on with him in the first place. But I was curious about how Sebastian would respond, so I looked over at him. He glanced at me; then his mouth curled into that slow, sexy smile of his. There was no disgust, no question in his eyes.

It almost looked like he was amused—or impressed?

What was his deal?

Sebastian sat there, waiting patiently for me to finish my shift, while I thought about how much I wished he had been a little bit jealous.

**15.** **WHEN WE GOT TO MY HOUSE AROUND**
three thirty, I knew my parents wouldn't be home. But they
would probably be back before my mom's Celebrate Christmas
rehearsal, which meant we didn't have a lot of time with the
house to ourselves. After my conversation with Mom about
Hunter that morning, I wasn't sure how she'd respond to
a strange boy showing up at our house for an afternoon of
chatting and cookies. I didn't really care, but when I told
Sebastian this, he grinned mischievously.

"I've never been on a snowmobile." He lifted his eyebrows.

"I saw yours parked out front—want to take me out for my first time? Get out of here for a while?"

"Are you sure you can handle it?" I asked. "I go fast."

"I'm sure you do." He laughed. "I'll be fine. Let's get out of here."

He'd given me a ride home, so we parked his car in our never-used barn to hide it from my parents' curious eyes. Then I loaned him a sweater from my dad's closet to give him an extra layer—the pretty-boy jacket wasn't going to cut it in below-freezing temps—and found a neck warmer he could borrow. After mixing up some hot chocolate in a thermos and throwing some licorice in a bag, we hopped on the love machine.

I was driving, with Sebastian behind me—his legs gripped my hips as we drove off across the fields and into the forest. I could feel the warmth of his thighs coming through the double layer of my pants and his and wondered what it would feel like to have his legs wrapped around me in a different setting.

We drove down an old walking trail that loops around the edge of town—it's often used for snowmobiling in the winter. A few miles away from my house the walking trail hooks up with some old cross-country ski trails, which hadn't been groomed yet for the season. We turned down a ski trail and pushed deeper into the woods, the dark canopy of trees making it feel like a winter wonderland in dusk light. I knew there was an old warming shack hidden deep in the woods—that was the destination I had in mind.

We could talk and drink hot chocolate, and I could boil over with lust and wanting and disappointment.

Sebastian's legs chilled as we drove deeper into the woods, and I could only feel the pressure on my hips now, not his heat. I knew he must be cold, since I was downright freezing. Just when I thought we would have to turn around and head back to my house to warm up, I spotted a clearing up ahead. The warming shack stood, small and deserted, beneath a circle of pine trees.

I drove the snowmobile up to the front of the little house and turned the motor off, hoping we'd get it started again later. It wasn't quite as unreliable as my car, but the love machine had been known to flake out before. Sebastian shook his legs as we climbed off the snowmobile—I guessed they were numb from the cold and wind. The warming shack was unlocked, but had obviously been deserted for a long, long time. It smelled stuffy when I opened the door, despite the biting chill, and cobwebs stretched across the inside of the door.

Sebastian followed me in, and we both stood in the middle of the little room letting our eyes adjust to the darkness so we could look around. It was tiny and barren and cold, and it looked a lot less comfortable than I had hoped it would. "We should get a fire going," Sebastian said, startling me. His voice echoed off the empty walls. "Someone was kind enough to cut some wood for us—do you think they left matches?"

I poked around the open room and found a box of matches inside a wooden box near the door. There was also an old blanket and some newspapers dating back to last winter. We stuffed the newspapers and some of the wood that was piled next to the door into the stove in the corner of the room. Once we had it lit, the heat poured over us almost immediately.

"Well," Sebastian said, settling in on the floor to open our thermos of hot cocoa. "Hopefully, I'll be able to feel my hands again someday."

"Are you cold?" I put on a silly, pitying voice and sat down with him. "Poor thing."

He smiled at me with that deliciously tempting mouth and nodded. "Freezing, actually."

I reached out to take his hands in mine. "Come on, hand them over." He studied me carefully as his hands reached out to meet mine, and in the dim light I thought I saw something strange pass across his face. Our hands touched, and I held his between mine, trying to help him warm up.

"You confuse me," he said as we sat there facing each other on the cold wooden floor, hands linked together.

"I confuse *you*? You confuse *me*."

"How's that?" He grinned. "I'm transparent." His right hand was squeezing mine a little—he was obviously defrosting. Was he just trying to get the blood flowing again? Or did the squeeze mean something?

"You're as transparent as a cement wall," I muttered. "Usually guys are pretty straightforward, but you're a major enigma."

He pulled his hands away from mine to pour each of us a cup of hot chocolate, then didn't give his hands back. I took a sip of my cocoa. It was lukewarm.

"We really shouldn't be out here together," he said, sending a chill down my spine. "I shouldn't have come."

"You seem like a perfectly normal guy until you say something like that," I responded coolly. "What's the deal?" He pulled a piece of licorice out of the bag and refused to look up at me. "I mean, I know I'm closed off, but you definitely take the cake. I'm a little nervous you're a convicted felon or something. Things you say are a little freakishly cryptic."

He looked up then, that same smile tugging at his mouth. "I'm not a felon. It's not funny to make jokes like that—what if I actually were a criminal? What would you say then? You're stuck out in the middle of the barren woods with me."

"I wasn't joking," I said seriously. "Some of the things you say truly make me think I should be afraid of you."

"You should probably trust your instincts." He leaned back on his arms, tilting his body away from me. The space between us was growing—we had started out holding hands, and now we were leaning away from each other with a mile of space dividing us in the still-chilly air. "I should trust mine and make you take me back home."

I shook my head. "That's fine—if you want me to take you home, I'm not going to force you to stay here." I was getting defensive and offended, and embarrassment was making my guard creep up.

"I want to stay," he said, doing that sexy growl thing again. "That's the problem."

I wanted to touch him so much it hurt. "You're not going to tell me you're a vampire, are you?"

He laughed hard. "Edward Cullen, yes."

"If you're not a vampire, I think we're okay. Werewolf?"

Things relaxed then, when he realized I understood his warning and I wanted to be there with him anyway. As long as he didn't pose any physical danger, I would stick with him. I didn't think he was a real threat—it seemed like there was some emotional danger, but *that* I could handle. I didn't think he understood that I didn't care about all of that. If I wanted a safe harbor of love and emotional togetherness, I could stick with Hunter. *Blech.*

"I saw you with a J. D. Salinger book at Matt's," I said, hoping to turn the conversation back on again. "I love *Nine Stories.*"

"I guess I should worry about your mental health more than mine, then, huh? Salinger is a little messed up."

I shrugged. "His stories make my life feel a lot more normal—these days, though, things in real life are a lot more fucked up than fiction."

Sebastian leaned forward again, his arms resting on his bent knees. "What could be more fucked up than fiction?" he asked.

It was the way his eyes searched mine that broke me down.

And that's when I decided to tell him everything. Everything that had been hidden behind that steely dam for eighteen years came spilling out in a rush.

"The most frightening thing is that he could die, and I'd be left with just my overbearing, unsatisfied mom," I said. Sebastian had listened without a single interruption as I'd told him how I'd found out about my dad's illness, and how we hadn't really talked about it as a family since. "I wish they trusted me enough to know that I should have been a part of it. I feel like a four-year-old being sent to bed while the adults talk about important things and eat ice cream."

He didn't say anything—not "maybe they didn't want to hurt your feelings" or "maybe they were afraid" or any other excuse to justify my parents' decisions. I appreciated that. Of course, Sadie hadn't made excuses for them either, but I'd stopped burdening her with my issues since she had her own problems to contend with.

I sighed and took a sip of my cold chocolate. Sebastian bit both ends off a licorice twist and handed it to me—a cherry straw to drink my cocoa. "The new drama is that my best friend is knocked up." I watched his reaction—mild surprise, but nothing over the top. "Go ahead and say it—classic small-town stupidity, right?"

"I was actually going to ask how she's doing."

"Not great. Freaked out."

"I bet you're right there with her," he guessed. I nodded, a lump rising in my throat as I thought about Sadie again. I hadn't talked to her since that morning. I hoped she was doing okay with Trav at their Christmas celebration. I wondered if she'd told him yet.

While we talked about Sadie, I watched Sebastian watching me—his eyes darting to my lips the way they always did, his body turned toward me, a captive listener. I told him all about Sadie and Trav's relationship, and how she was acting so strong but was clearly still so fragile. And then my dad . . .

hiding his fear from me so I wouldn't be affected by it. Then me, keeping my guard up to hold myself together.

"But I *am* scared," I said finally, admitting what I hadn't said aloud to anyone—ever, maybe. At least not since I was a child and afraid of the armyworms that hung from our trees in the summer. "I don't know what I want to do with my life, and I see all this stuff *happening* to everyone around me, and I feel like I need to get it together. My life is about wanting to have sex and running and surviving my time in Milton—it all feels so trivial and small and petty."

I started to cry. Not the sobbing, hysterical, blubbery kind, just sort of a cleansing purge that left cold, wet streaks on my cheeks.

He pulled me against him then—the warmth of the fire was dying down, and we'd already put the last log in the stove. I was starting to get cold, but I didn't want to leave, not now. "I don't know what to say," he murmured into my hair. He went with: "You're freezing."

"I'm okay." I was responding to both his comments with one glib line. Sebastian held me tighter. I reminded myself not to read anything into it—he was just comforting me, trying to make me feel better about my fucked-up life.

I was just about to tell him he didn't have to do that—that I could handle it on my own; I was just venting—when he leaned in from over my shoulder and tilted my face toward his. His eyes searched mine and then he rested his cheek against mine. His arms were curled around me, holding me hostage.

I almost exploded with desire—until I realized it was such a warm, comforting friend thing to do that I just couldn't risk touching him more than that. I was suddenly crippled with an uncomfortable vulnerability, a raw, naked feeling that was making me cautious and scared—it's funny how showing my emotional innards was far more daunting than taking off my bra. I'd opened myself up to him, and it was holding me back now, making me feel less aggressive and confident. "I've never really talked about me as much as I just did," I said. His cheek was still pressed into mine. "I'm sorry."

He pulled away. "Why would you say that?"

"I—I'm just surprised at how out there I feel right now. You know these secrets about me, and it's awkward. I guess you weren't really wrong when you guessed I shut people out." Even as I said that, I could feel myself pulling away, putting the game face back on. He had an advantage, and I wasn't comfortable with that. The rational part of my brain was telling me to shut my mouth. "I'm just waiting to regret telling you so much."

His silence freaked me out. His cheek was no longer touching mine, and I knew I'd screwed up. My body stiffened under his arms, scared of opening up any further.

Until he said: "I like getting to know you like that." His arms tightened, holding me closer. "I bet not a lot of people do."

"You'd be right about that," I said quietly.

"I don't usually care as much as I do right now." He shifted, and pulled a pack of gum out of his pocket, offering me a piece—it broke the intensity a little bit, which relaxed me. When I put the stick of cinnamon gum in my mouth, it mixed with the flavor of the chocolate and licorice, a sweet and spicy combination that lit my tongue on fire. "There's something about you that makes me want to listen, to actually care."

"Well, aren't you Mr. Sensitive?" I teased.

"Not usually," he admitted. "But tonight." And that's when he put his cheek back against mine. I felt his fuzzy facial hair slide against my cheek as he brought his lips closer to mine, though we were still just cheek to cheek. Was this still just comforting? Was it possible he was still trying to keep me away when he was tempting me like this?

And then, suddenly, his mouth was on mine, and the fire I'd felt on my tongue was on my lips. The kiss almost knocked me backward, it hit me so hard. I was still so vulnerable, and it felt like we were connected in a million places. I don't know how we got there, but we were suddenly lying on the cold, hard floor, and his hand was on my neck, pulling my face in toward his. I was out of breath and surprised and overwhelmed. Nothing had prepared me for this kind of want—it wasn't just physical. I wanted to touch him in so many ways. I wanted to explore him.

Sebastian made me *feel* in a way I never had before.

His hands held mine as we kissed, and I was torn between the passion of wanting to keep going and my own fears. He'd transitioned from hot potential fuck to an emotional crutch, I realized, and I didn't know what to make of that. I felt so connected to him, and it scared me.

After a momentary pause I relaxed into him, letting his mouth take me away from everything. I was wrapped up in him. Then I giggled when his gum transferred from his mouth to mine, and he pulled back. He put his hands on my cheeks, and moved them down to feel my belly, which was slightly exposed beneath the hem of my sweater.

I realized then that I was shaking, shivering with cold. "We have to get you home," he announced. "Your hands are like ice."

"I'm fine." I knew he was right, but I didn't want the day to end. It was dark outside, so I knew it must be past dinnertime, but there was nothing I needed to get home to.

He shook his head. "I don't believe that," he said. "Let's get back—get you in a hot bath or something to warm you up."

Two hours earlier I would have said: "Are you going to join me?" But now I just nodded. The fear of rejection was too overwhelming to put myself out there like that. I just had to trust that he felt the way I did, and let things develop the way they were supposed to. We'd get there—right?

We hopped on my snowmobile, and it started easily. The drive back seemed long, but his arms around me had a different feeling this time. They weren't just holding on to keep him on the back of the snowmobile—they were wrapped around me the way they'd been wrapped around me back in the warming shack, holding me close. As we pulled the snowmobile into the barn, right next to his car, his mouth came up to my ear and whispered, "I don't know what to make of you."

"Good," I said, turning around on the seat to face him. "Then we're even."

He kissed me again, and we sat there on the snowmobile making out in the shelter of the barn. It wasn't until both of us were frozen to the core—our lips the only heat between us—that we finally pulled apart. I watched as he drove away, down the long, snowy road.

I knew then that I was in deep.

 **CHRISTMAS EVE WAS ... DIFFERENT,**
to say the least.

If I remember only one thing about the Celebrate Christmas performance at church, it will be that Hunter Johnson got a boner during the nativity skit.

Yes, there's context.

Because we were spending Christmas Eve with the Johnsons, my mom thought it would be fun for my dad and me to join Hunter and his dad during services (the moms sit with the rest of the choir up front, on the church's only cushioned benches). With my dad in charge of getting us there on time, we were more than a little late. He'd been in a haze of distraction lately and was lucky I'd put an emergency backup tie in my coat pocket, since he forgot to put one on. Mere moments before the service was set to begin, my dad and I snuck in the side door and searched for any open pews.

Lucky for us Hunter and his dad were sitting together in the back row, right on the outer aisle. The rest of the church was full, so after a few seconds of rushed discussion, the dads thought it would be nice for me to sit with Hunter while they found themselves a spot out in the lobby to listen to the service on the TVs.

And that's how it came about that I was left alone with Hunter Johnson for the first time since our last afternoon together. Things were going along just fine—church keeps you pretty occupied, thus avoiding uncomfortable conversation—when suddenly, as we stood there singing a song, Hunter reached behind me and squeezed my ass cheek. Not just an *oops, I meant to grab the songbook* sort of butt-brush, but a whole-hand grab, complete with a little rubbing.

"Um, hi?" I said, trying not to raise my voice in church.

"Hi, yourself," Hunter murmured back, his eyes all sultry and hopeful. We were on the last verse of "Silent Night," so things were sufficiently noisy around us and no one could hear the conversation. Nor could anyone see that his hand remained on my butt. That was the fortunate thing about the back row.

Where did this guy come from? I wondered. There we stood—Hunter's hand on my ass while we sang classic carols, watching people act out Jesus' birth scene. "Care to take your hand off my rear end?" I whispered, when he didn't politely remove it.

"Nope," he said proudly. So I put my own hand behind me and forcefully removed it for him. The congregation moved onto an off-tune rendition of "Joy to the World." And that's when I spotted it: the Christmas Boner. There it was, standing proudly under the thin fabric of his dress pants, starting our Christmas festivities off right.

There were no other attempted come-ons during church, for which I was relieved. I didn't understand what Hunter was doing, since he knew we weren't going to be boyfriend-girlfriend. I was sad I couldn't give him that. I glanced over at him during the offering and noticed how plain and simple and uncomplicated he was: a nice choice, a safe choice.

But I hated myself when I was with him. I hated the life he represented.

As we left our pew, Hunter followed close behind me,

his arm floating behind my back as though he were ushering me out of church. Almost like we were a couple—an old, boring, married couple. I hoped he would find someone nice and stable someday, a girl who could be as nice to him as he would be to her: a girl who had something to give, a girl without an agenda, a girl who didn't play him for a fool. A girl unlike me.

The church lobby was packed. Nearly everyone in town came out for Christmas services. No one wanted to get tongues wagging by skipping. The choir was busy accepting congratulations on a successful show, and the nativity performers were thanking everyone for coming.

Tina Zander, who was anything but a Virgin, had played this year's Mary (a highly coveted role, since it is usually a precursor to winning the lead in the spring musical at school). It all had a nice, ironic feel—especially when Vic went up to congratulate her by squeezing her tit in front of half the congregation.

My dad and I reunited in the corner of the lobby, away from the hubbub. I looked around for Sadie, and when I noticed that her parents were there with only Jeremy, I panicked. I'd been trying to call her all day to find out how her eve of Christmas Eve with Trav had gone, but she hadn't picked up her phone.

My parents had refused to let me drive anywhere all day (the roads were icy—light snow had been falling since day-break, and the salt trucks couldn't keep up). Which meant I had had to resort to trying to get Sadie via cell or text. She wasn't answering either, and now that she'd ditched church, I knew I had to worry. I resolved to try to sneak out after dinner somehow, even if it meant dragging Hunter along for the ride, to try to get to her house.

Dad nudged me then, and we went together to tell my mom how lovely she'd sounded. Mom often talked about how there were some real stinker voices in the choir, and how their director specifically miked up the people who made them sound like pros. I'd heard Mom sing at home and really doubted she was one of the director's chosen ones, but she was sure her lovely voice carried across the church for all to enjoy. We played along. This performance was the highlight of Mom's year.

Just as I was pinching my dad's elbow, eager to get in the car and get back home to crack into his famous Christmas meatballs, I noticed Sebastian and his dad passing through the church lobby. Sebastian's dad stopped to greet a few people, while Sebastian just stood there looking hot and out of place. After our day together yesterday I didn't really want to see him here, mixed in with my regular life like this. I didn't want him to be a part of Milton. Didn't want him to ooze into the lameness of my day-to-day.

Apparently, he felt the same.

Because when he and his dad passed me a few moments later on their way out of church, he didn't say a word. He looked right at me, acknowledged my existence with a curt nod, and walked past. His dad, noticing Sebastian's nod in my direction, Merry-Christmased us, and that was the warmest part of the entire greeting from the Bowman twosome. I was smiling like a fool until I realized Sebastian had passed—gone. As though we were almost strangers.

Had I totally fabricated our connection? Was I so desperate to be with him that I pretended the closeness had existed? Had it meant nothing to him? Suddenly I understood his warning. He'd pulled me close, and now he was pushing me away. He had warned me to stay away, and I'd totally failed to keep my distance.

Kiss it, asshole, I cursed silently, resolving to spit in his burger if he ever came into Matt's again. And then the hurt hit. Like the power of our first kiss, the pain of knowing I'd lost him almost knocked me over. I pulled my dad out the door and hustled to the car. I didn't want to be surrounded by the cheer of church and my mom's perky voice when I felt this kind of despair. I realized there had been a reason for me to feel vulnerable in the woods—it had all meant nothing to him, and I'd spilled my soul.

I stared blindly out the window as we drove through town. I was numb and cold and hurt. The snow was coming at us quickly, little shards of ice that were stopped by the windshield. "It's slick," my dad said, and I grunted in response.

"I'm hungry for those meatballs," he tried again, a little while later. Once again I said nothing, just stared at those icy snowflakes coming at me like swords. I felt the car slip on the icy road a few times, but I barely even noticed. I just wanted to get home, to spend the night with the Johnsons pretending life was good. Clearly, that was the best strategy, since opening yourself up to honest feelings just brought more hurt, as I'd learned tonight.

Less than a half mile from our house the headlights illuminated a herd of deer standing in the middle of the road. I could tell my dad was watching me, trying to figure out why I was so sulky, and his eyes weren't watching what they should be. I was so out of it that I didn't realize I needed to warn him until those deer were right in front of the car. Hearing my shout, my dad looked ahead, then swore before swerving. There was a loud thud as we flew off the road, taking one of the deer with us. I saw the snowbank fly up at us in slow motion, the fluff of fresh snow coming up over the car like a waterfall.

And then everything went still. I didn't have to do a body check to know that everything was still in place and unharmed. I knew I was fine. But when I looked over at my dad, there was blood on his face. That's when I started to cry. It was only a moment of panic that left me sitting there sobbing, and then I unbuckled myself from my seat belt to get to my dad. "Dad!" I called. "Dad! Are you okay?"

Desperate for him to stir, I was hit with the irony. I'd been so scared of his cancer, and now he was going to be taken from me like this? I looked at him lying there, silent and still. His head was bleeding, and I realized then that he hadn't been wearing his seat belt. He always complained that it was too tight, too restrictive on his chubby belly. I could hear him now: "My tummy will work like a cushion if I ever get in an accident—I'll bounce right off the wheel." But he hadn't bounced right off—he'd hit the wheel with his head, and now he was slumped against it, and I was scared.

I touched his cheek and spotted the deer, callously staring into the back of our car, watching us with its dead eyes. I hated that deer, and I hated myself for having wished I was part of a different family. I choked under my tears and begged for another chance to tell my dad I loved him.

It had only been a few seconds, really, when my dad blinked and lifted his head to look at me. "Holy shit," he murmured. "Are you okay, pumpkin?"

I nodded, still crying. "I love you, Dad."

"It feels like everything is still in one piece," he mused.

"Not quite." I took off my glove and dabbed at the blood on his face. "One of the deer didn't make it. He's out back." I gestured out the back window, where that creepy deer was still watching us.

And then the insanity began. Hunter and his dad, who had been following us home, pulled over and jumped out of their car to find us inside the snowbank. Hunter called 911 while his dad started digging us out with a shovel from their trunk, all the while instructing us to stay put in case there was a neck injury. Just when they'd dug us out enough that the car doors would open, the EMT showed up and insisted that both my dad and I needed to come with them. Ethan Zupancich, who'd graduated three years ago, helped me out of the car and onto a stretcher that he and another guy loaded into the back of the ambulance.

I glanced at Hunter as I was carried past the two Johnson men. His face wore the exact same expression as his dad's, and I could picture what he would be like in twenty years: stable, dependable, unchanged.

My dad was loaded in next to me a few seconds later. Just as the doors to the back of the county ambulance swung closed, Mr. Johnson popped his head in to check on us one last time. At least I thought that's what he was doing—until he asked my dad, "Are you going to keep that deer? If you're not, mind if I take the meat?"

 **17.** **CHRISTMAS EVE DINNER WAS SERVED**
on a tray—a brown plastic tray with a small Santa bobblehead
sitting next to the Jell-O. My mom, dad, and I were all settled
comfortably in a room at the Flanders Hospital, enjoying the
last few hours of our Christmas Eve watching the local news
report on Santa's whereabouts. Apparently, he was somewhere
over Madison, Wisconsin, and would surely be in Northland
with plenty of time to make his annual toy deliveries via
chimney chute.

"Do you think Santa knows I'm here?" I wondered aloud

from my slumped position on the lounger in the corner of the room. "They always say he can find you anywhere. Can he find me at the hospital?"

I caught my parents exchanging a look. As if they thought I was asking a serious question. My mom comforted me by saying, "Sweetie, I think Santa will leave some things at our house for you. He knows we'll all be home soon."

"Phew," I muttered. "That was a close one."

Mom excused herself into the hall then, probably to call Miriam Johnson and ask her to stuff the stockings at our house with the bags of crap she had bought that were, at present, inexpertly hidden inside her closet.

Dad looked over at me from his bed, where he was hooked up to an IV of fluids. He'd had to get six stitches for the head wound, and they were keeping him overnight for monitoring. I was off the hook. "You feeling okay?" I asked. This was still new for me, asking how people were feeling—I was scared of what the answer might be, and frightened about how I would respond if the answer was anything other than yes. I was shaken, both from the accident and from my encounter with Sebastian. (Physically, I was just fine.)

"Oh, I'm all right. Do you want some ham?" He was cutting bits of dry meat on the hospital tray and offered me a bite off his fork.

"Um . . ." I pretended to think about it. ". . . nope." Then I pulled out the bag of M&M's I'd snuck from the vending machine while my parents were signing admission papers.

"Hand it over," my dad demanded.

I looked up, aghast. I couldn't believe he'd deny me chocolate after driving me into a snowbank. On Christmas Eve, no less. But when I saw his face and his wiggling fingers, I could see that he meant for me to share. I opened up my pocket and pulled out a second bag—even though we weren't the perfect family match in many ways, we did share a love of candy. Dad had the tummy to prove it. I'd wisely bought two bags.

"Are you sure *you're* okay?" Dad asked for the gazillionth time. "I feel terrible, Chastity."

I groaned. "Dad, it's not your fault. Get over it. I'm fine, I swear." I *was* fine, on the outside—but everything else was eating me up, and I didn't know why I couldn't say that. Why I wouldn't say that.

"I'm sorry about hiding my cancer from you too, baby."

I popped a handful of M&M's in my mouth and nodded. "S'okay."

"It's not," he said. "I lied, and I lost your trust."

"It doesn't feel great to find out I'm not considered mature enough to be a participating member of the family," I admitted. "That sucks."

"I know you don't want to hear my excuses, but I do want you to know that I think the world of you and your confidence, and you deserved to know. I was scared—I was somehow kidding myself that the cancer would go away if I didn't tell you about it." He sounded a lot like me. "I should have been honest."

I moved my chair to be right next to his bed. Then I laid my head against his big, puffy, chocolaty tummy (he'd dropped an M&M, which had melted down the side of the scratchy hospital blanket—with enough body heat M&M's *do* melt in places other than your mouth). "I need to tell you something, Dad." I guess it was the spirit of Christmas coming over me. "I lied about applying to the U—I haven't applied to any colleges yet. I don't think I want to go."

After a brief pause, wherein I held my breath and questioned my decision to spill it, my dad started laughing. His tummy was rolling under me, shaking with belly laughs. "Ooh-hoo, your mother is going to freak out," he said finally.

"You're not mad?" I asked, turning my head to look at him. "Don't you think I'm a huge, lying disappointment?"

"I can't say I'm thrilled," he admitted. "I was excited that you were going to have opportunities I didn't. But it's your call, pumpkin. I can't make your life choices for you—God knows, your mother makes mine for me, and look where it's gotten me?" He was making a joke, but I saw a lot of truth in what he'd said. I knew my dad wasn't unhappy about it—he'd picked my mom and had to have known the strings that were attached to that commitment. "I'm sure you don't want my advice, but I'm happy to talk about it if you want to. . . ."

"Actually, Dad"—I took a deep breath—"I'd really like that." He adjusted on his bed, sitting up to push his tray away toward his feet. He looked ready to talk now. "I've sort of been thinking about AmeriCorps—something like that could get me out, doing something fun and good? Make a little money to live on while I explore and just *live* for a while."

"That would suit you."

"We'll see," I mused, not wanting to commit to any kind of agenda yet. "Maybe we can save this conversation for home?" He nodded and patted my head. It felt great. I smiled up at him, realizing that maybe I wasn't a huge disappointment. "Do you mind if we keep this confession just between us?" I suggested. "Maybe until the New Year?"

"I'm okay with that." And so it was that my dad and I formed a tiny little bond over secrets and lies and chocolate. We ate the rest of our M&M's quickly, trying to stuff them all in before Mom could sniff them out and confiscate them.

The door to our room opened and Mom poked her head

in. She was too smiley. "Guess what I have for you two?" she singsonged.

I hoped the answer was chocolate cake or something equally tasty, but when Mom opened the door all the way, the Johnsons were standing on the other side, glowing in the hospital light. "Helloooooo!" Miriam Johnson called out. "I hope you're feeling okay, because we brought Christmas to you!"

Hunter and his parents bustled into the hospital room then, surrounding my dad's bed. They had brought a bowl of meatballs (thank you!), some of Miriam's infamous(ly bad) plum tarts, and a heap of mystery meat on a plate. Hunter stared at his shoes and not at me. He was probably wondering if maybe the Lord had been punishing him for putting his hand on my ass in church by getting me into a car accident. *As if.*

My mom looked around the room, thrilled. "Isn't this a nice surprise?"

"Wow. Thanks." I popped a meatball into my mouth. The plate of mystery meat was placed haphazardly at the end of my dad's bed, with a steamy piece of plastic wrap pulled tight over the top. I took a closer look before asking, "What's that?"

Mr. Johnson clapped loudly. He's one of those guys—the kind who's so awkward in social situations that when he finally gets a chance to talk, he is loud and irritating. "Venison!" he guffawed. "I was running low, but I thought we could enjoy the last package in the deep freeze since we got a fresh load tonight. You hit that sucker dead on—we'll get a lot of meat out of that girl."

While everyone talked about the virtue of roadkill, I excused myself to the hallway under the guise of using the restroom. There were big signs in all the hospital rooms instructing you to turn off your cell phone, which I had, but I really needed to try to get in touch with Sadie. When I turned my phone on out in the lobby, I found I had two texts.

The first, from Sebastian. It said, *I can explain. Please give me that chance.* My finger hovered over the delete button, then hit save instead. I moved to the next one.

It was from Sadie, less than an hour ago: *I know it's Xmas— but can you come over as soon as you get this? I need help.*

Oh, God. I swallowed. I had to get to her. Because it was so late, I texted her to say I was on my way. But how? There was no way I was going to get out of family Christmas dinner around my dad's hospital bed. It seemed wrong that I was even considering an escape. But my best friend needed me, and I needed to be there for her. I considered the options:

One of our cars was totaled, and probably still in the ditch. It most certainly wasn't parked in the hospital lot and available for a speedy getaway. Using the car my mom had driven would involve stealing her keys and stranding her at the hospital for the night—and I needed to get out of there without inspiring any questions.

I could ask Hunter to take me. *Um, no.* The more I leaned on him, the more I gave him the wrong idea, and he deserved better.

My fingers hit dial before I'd fully made up my mind. "Sebastian?" I said, cold and formal. "Can you pick me up from the hospital in Flanders?"

He agreed immediately, no questions asked, despite the fact that it was Christmas Eve and he was probably eating mac and cheese in a cup with his dad in their weird little living room. I went back to the hospital room for a while to wait. It would take at least half an hour for Sebastian to get there, and I needed to come up with some excuse for leaving.

We sang some songs (two church choir moms—what else could be expected?) and continued to watch the news. I caught Hunter staring at me when we sang "Joy to the World," sending me *Be strong; I'm here for you* vibes with his eyes. I lifted my eyebrows at him, as if to say: *Enough, pal. Time to give up already.*

I excused myself a few minutes later and decided to just leave. I needed to get out of there, and I couldn't deal with the conversation about why and where I was going. I knew it was the cowardly thing to do, but it was my only choice.

I left a note for my parents at the nurses' station, telling them I had called a friend to give me a ride home and that I'd see them in the morning. I couldn't tell them the truth. So I did what I had to do.

I climbed into the passenger seat of Sebastian's dad's car. He didn't drive off immediately, so I reached over and put the shifter in drive to show him I didn't have time to waste looking at each other tonight. "Just go. I need to get back to Milton," I said. Then, "Thanks for picking me up."

"Everything okay?" he asked softly.

"It's Sadie," I said, then turned to look out the window. "I don't know yet."

He drove slowly, on account of the snow. "Why were you at the hospital?"

"Car accident."

"Who?"

"Me. And my dad."

"Oh, God. Chaz, are you okay?" He looked over at me.

"Can you keep your eyes on the road, please? That's how I got into one accident tonight." I could smell the sweetness of his cinnamon gum, and it brought back a wave of memories from the day before. I felt sick.

"Chaz, listen, I'm sorry I didn't say anything to you earlier tonight."

"Yeah, me too."

The radio was playing Christmas music. I tried to sink into the sounds of the season and tune out this conversation. But he obviously wanted to talk. "I told you things are tricky with me."

"I guess so." I wasn't sulking. Just didn't want him to think I cared.

"There's a lot of stuff going on." He sighed. "I . . ."

I leaned my head against the window, letting the cool glass numb a piece of me. "Don't worry about it, okay? I get it."

"I'm pretty sure you don't." He started to look at me again; I could see it out of the corner of my eye. Then his head turned back to the road again, just as quickly. "I want to explain. It's hard for me. I don't—"

"Don't bother." For some reason, saying that made my stomach ache. I could feel him there next to me, and I *did* want him to bother. I wanted him to care enough that he would explain, would tell me something that would make me understand why he'd hurt me like that. But even more I wanted an explanation from myself as to why I'd let myself fall so hard that a single brush-off from a guy I apparently barely knew could hurt me so badly.

We had just passed the SPEED LIMIT 30 sign that announced the Milton city limits. I directed him to Sadie's house, and when we pulled up in front, he put the car in park. "Please, Chaz," he said—levelly, not pleading, not begging—"don't let this thing between us go. Tomorrow? We can go back out in the woods? You look so cute on a snowmobile."

"Don't push it," I threatened. Then I nodded. "Not tomorrow. The twenty-sixth. You should be with your dad on Christmas." He nodded back. "You have to promise me one thing." I wanted to end on a light note—I didn't want him to think of me as some mopey, high-maintenance diva. I waited for him to agree, then said, "You will be forced to consume many strips of roadkill jerky. That's your penance for being a total asshole today." Then, finally, I smiled at him. "Merry Christmas, Sebastian."

**18.** **I SNUCK AROUND BACK, THROUGH**
the snow, to Sadie's window. Her light was on, even though
by now it was close to midnight. My feet were freezing—
I was still wearing my church outfit, and my shoes were still
damp from climbing out of the ditch through the snow after
the accident.

Her curtain pulled back, and she motioned me to the back
door, through the kitchen. She was standing on the other side
by the time I got there. We crept into her room, and once the
door was safely closed, I hugged her close.

"It's over, Chaz," Sadie said, curling up on her bed in a little ball.

I stared at her. "What's over?"

"The baby. It's gone."

"Gone?"

"It fell out."

My eyes widened. "You had a miscarriage?"

She started crying then. "Yes," she blubbered. "I was going to keep it, Chaz. We were going to keep it."

"Are you okay, Sade? Do you need to go to the doctor?" I wondered how many rooms my family and friends could fill at Flanders Hospital tonight. "You need to see someone." I took a breath. "How do you know?"

"I've gone through half a bag of those pads with wings since dinner. The extra-long kind my mom keeps in her bathroom. It's a lot of blood, Chaz." She sobbed. "My baby."

Oh, God. I racked my brain, trying to figure out what to say. "Are you okay?" I asked again. I swallowed back the relief that was flooding over me, realizing it was all over. It made me sick that I felt the way I did, but things suddenly seemed so much simpler for Sadie.

She nodded, chewing her lower lip. "We were going to keep it, Chaz. I talked to Trav last night, and"—Sadie cut off again, choked up with tears—"he thought we could do it. He was actually excited about it. We talked about how we could live with his aunt down in Minneapolis, and I could still go to Macalester, and we would get married. This summer, maybe, after my birthday."

I thought about how crazy that all sounded. Out loud I said, "I'm glad he was supportive. Trav's a sweet guy."

Sadie smiled sadly. "We had it all planned out."

"I'm sure you did." I walked over to sit next to her. It was terrible, what was happening to Sadie, but I couldn't help but feel some fear about what she was saying. She'd been so excited about her dorm, and her plan to go to St. Louis for the architecture program. How do you move to another state with a three-year-old?

I wondered: *Am I still supporting my best friend's choices when I'm feeling so much relief about her* need *to choose being taken away?*

"I'm glad you and Trav talked about it," I said, trying to make my tone comforting. "Does he know this happened?"

"No." Sadie said. "I can't tell him on Christmas. He'll be so disappointed."

I watched her face, so solid in its resolve and confidence. I knew she was crumbling inside, so I said, "You know this isn't your fault, right?"

She chewed her lip, biting back the tears. "I guess."

"It's not, Sade."

"I feel like God is punishing me for going to the clinic when I found out. Like he knew I was thinking about getting rid of it, so he just took it away." She cried into my shoulder, my sweet Sadie. "Took my baby away, because I didn't deserve it. Didn't want it enough. I got to keep it long enough to realize I wanted it, that we needed it, and then—"

"Oh, honey." I held her; then I cried too. "Please don't blame yourself—it doesn't work that way. And Trav will understand." We sat like that for a long time, me holding her, Sadie holding her stomach. Finally, I said, "We do need to bring you in to the doctor."

She nodded. "I'll have Trav bring me after Christmas. After I've told him—I want him to be there."

"Okay," I agreed. That seemed right. After all, if they were talking about marriage and kids and moving in together, they probably should do this kind of thing as a couple. As I thought about that, I truly realized—for the first time, I guess—that after high school things would change. I'd always known this in theory, but I guess I'd never really thought about it as a collection of specifics and how it would change things with my best friend.

Sadie would have Trav to help her through her issues. My parents would have each other. And I'd be jumping into a world full of strangers, forced to figure it all out from scratch. Much as I didn't fit in here in Milton, at least I knew how everything worked. And everyone in town had known me so long that it didn't really matter that they didn't really *know* me. They knew enough about me that I wasn't a total stranger here.

But out in the real world, away from here, with new people, I was going to have to open myself up, or I'd be alone. A stranger in a strange land. I suddenly thought of Sebastian, and how he'd been the first person aside from Sadie that I'd shared myself with—those deep-down, private parts of myself that I wanted to keep covered up. Then, instantly, I thought about his blow-off after church.

Even while I questioned our "connection," I knew I had to give Sebastian a chance to explain. It was so tempting to close up, clamlike, and hide. But I'd felt safe with him, and I knew I needed to open myself up to disappointment in order to find out why he'd been brought into my life, to figure out what it meant to feel this way about someone. Sex wasn't even driving this anymore.

Sadie sighed then, and from the pace of her breathing, I knew she was asleep. I seemed to have this effect on her lately. I lay her down against her pillow, flipped off the light, and settled in next to her for the night.

Lying there in the dark, I wondered if my parents were

worried about me. I decided to text my dad—I owed it to him after taking off the way I had. Secrets and lies had gotten us nowhere. And after the accident he would probably worry even if I were curled up at the foot of his bed. I sent him a text letting him know I was at Sadie's, that we were together tonight. I told him I was safe.

He texted back almost instantly to say: *ok, mery Christmas pumplin.* (Dad was still getting the hang of text messaging.)

Then I let myself drift off to sleep, and I prayed in my own special way for visions of sugarplums to dance in my head.

I woke with a throbbing pain shooting down my neck. When I stood up and looked in the mirror, I had a faint—but blossoming—bruise on my collarbone from where the seat belt had dug in against my shoulder during the impact of the accident. My eyes were sunken and dark from lack of sleep. I looked a mess.

Sadie stirred a few minutes after I woke up and told me I should stay for Christmas morning. Realizing I had nowhere else to go (Mom was sure to be at the hospital with Dad), I was grateful for the togetherness that Sadie's family oozed. Even her brother, Jeremy, was charming, I realized, when you had no home to go to yourself, and any brother was better than no one at all.

They were all very sweet to me and gasped appropriately through my story of the accident. But I still felt out of place, like an imposter, when everyone started opening their presents and I was just sitting there. I was like a loaf of Nonna's Christmas bread—the kind of thing people feel like they have to eat but no one really wants to waste the calories on.

Right after their big pancake breakfast I excused myself to shower, and I prepared to leave. That was when I realized I had no way to get out of there. I had hoped to sneak out unobtrusively, but someone was going to have to give me a lift. Sadie was still in her pajamas, but she threw on her parka and offered me a ride home anyway. "Okay," I reluctantly agreed.

In the car she was very quiet. "I'm going to call Trav tonight. I'll tell him what happened, and he can take me to the doctor tomorrow. I might have him bring me back to the clinic so the bill won't show up on my parents' insurance. Maybe I'll talk to the doctor about going on the pill."

"If you need me, just let me know. I'm yours."

"Thanks." She drove down my driveway and pulled up at the front door. "Can you believe how much has happened over break?"

I smiled at her—a natural reflex, not a reflection of any kind of pleasure or mirth—then shook my head. "Are you sure you're gonna be okay?"

She nodded. "I'll be fine. We've really changed, haven't we? Look at us, dealing with big stuff."

"Big stuff," I echoed, then gave her a hug and went inside. As I walked up to the door, all I could think was . . . *but have I changed?*

Feeling the false smile still on my face—frighteningly similar to the one I'd seen on my mom so many times before—and the unspoken fear that was sinking over me while I outwardly "dealt with" everything going down around me, I knew I had the answer:

Not so much.

**19.** **"I DOUBT YOU'RE INTERESTED IN**
excuses, right?" This was the first thing Sebastian said to me
when I opened my front door the next day. He was standing
there on my doorstep, surrounded by swirling snow, sporting
a floppy knit winter hat and looking adorably goofy.

God, how I wanted him. But I had to get over it. "That
is correct."

"And clever conversation will probably only take me so
far?" His eyes glinted, a troublemaker through and through.

"Not far at all. You've reached the end of that road, I'm

afraid." I invited him inside and handed him a box full of venison jerky. The snow had been coming down since Christmas Eve, so there was no way we were going to get my piece of shit snowmobile to carry us out into the woods as planned—it was a miracle his car had made it out to my place at all. Now that he was here, we were stuck chilling in my basement. It felt wrong, somehow, bringing him into my house. But we didn't have any other options, so Sebastian followed me down the stairs and into the family den.

I grabbed the remote and put a movie on for background noise—something with Audrey Hepburn that would certainly make me feel bad about the absence of real romance in my life. I watched pretty little Audrey traipsing down a cobblestone road with an adorable short haircut and a smile. "Frankly, I don't know why I'm even hanging out with you again," I said. "Clearly, I'm just bored." It was the day after Christmas, and my parents were on their way back down to Minneapolis to squeeze in some sort of clinical research appointments in while my dad had days off from the bank—so I was on my own for the night. My parents had gotten home from the hospital so late last night that we hadn't even opened Christmas gifts yet.

"If I were to kiss you, what would happen then?" He said this through a mouth full of tough jerky.

Let's find out, I thought, wishing he would just do that. Out loud I answered, "I'd probably slap you. Much as I enjoyed kissing you the other day, I'm not falling for your bullshit again." He looked hurt—good. "Fool me once, shame on you. Fool me twice, shame on me. I'm not stupid—I know you're just a player. Which wouldn't bother me, were it not for the fact that you put on this big show about actually caring."

"I'm not playing you." He sighed.

My heart skipped a beat. "I thought I'd made it pretty fucking clear that you didn't need to get all emotional with me. I would have been perfectly content just hooking up—hanging out for a while—but you kept asking questions and making me talk." I realized I sounded sort of shrill and majorly whiny. But I couldn't stop. "I would have been happy to skip over all the emotional bullshit and just kiss."

"That's what makes you so fantastic," he said, setting the deer meat on the floor next to the couch. "But I love talking about your 'emotional bullshit,' Chaz. That's what's messing me up."

I tucked my feet up in front of me, physically walling myself off from him. "Why are you here?" I came out with it bluntly. "How am *I* messing *you* up?"

He ran a hand through his hair, and the way one piece dropped back down over his eyes twisted me up into knots and bows and made me feel like screaming and pounding my feet on the couch. I was smitten. A smitten kitten. Yet I hated him for messing with me. He reached out to take my hand, and I pulled it away, tucked it under my ass. He'd have to dig in and fish for it if he wanted it that bad.

"I've played a lot of girls, Chaz." He stretched out on the other section of my L-couch, his fingers fiddling with a loose thread on one of the throw pillows. "In fact that's sort of why I'm in Milton right now."

I waited, and when he didn't say anything more, I asked, "Is this your big emotional moment? You're going to break down and get all weepy, making me feel bad for you because you've played a lot of girls?"

"Come on! This is hard for me. You're making it worse." He was laughing, which made my insides feel like I'd eaten a tub of frosting—all giddy and jittery and a little nauseous. I loved to make him laugh, but it made me sick that I'd fallen so hard—that I lived for his laugh.

"So what is it? You get off on a girl crying?" I was semi-serious now. "Because I don't especially like to open up to people, and you did something sneaky and tricky that made me fall for your wily ways and tell you things about myself that I didn't particularly want to tell. You tricked me into thinking you cared. And now I'm really, really pissed at myself for being such a sucker."

That's when he moved over onto my section of the couch and grabbed my hand out from under my ass. He held it in his own. "You aren't a sucker. God, Chaz, it's not like that. It's so different with you. I'm scared of you."

"Good."

"Yeah, I guess it is good. It's making me feel bad about who I am. Who I was."

"Poor you."

"I've really screwed up, Chaz. A lot of times." He held my hand in his, and I let him. He looked less ruggedly confident than I'd seen him before. "The girl I was with before I came here for Christmas—I really fucked her up. I don't know how it happened, but I guess I didn't handle things the right way. She has issues—"

"Because of you?" I broke in. "Aren't you giving yourself an awful lot of credit? You're so hot and desirable that girls are just literally melting and falling apart at your feet?"

"Her name is Elizabeth. I suspected she had fallen hard, but I just wanted to have fun." He let my hand go. "But it wasn't like that for her. She thought we were something—when I hooked up with another girl at a party during Thanksgiving break and then broke things off with Elizabeth a few days later . . . she just fell apart. It was the same with Sabrina, who I hung out with before Elizabeth. And Jessie, before her.

It's always been fun for me—they were all hot, sweet—but for them it was love or something, I guess." He broke off again, fiddling with the pillow so hard that he pulled the thread loose and opened a hole in the fabric. "A part of me knows it's happening, every single time, but I can't stop myself."

I watched him, fascinated. It was like watching a documentary on assholes.

The kind of guy I'd never fallen for before.

The kind of guy I never should fall for.

The kind of guy I felt myself falling for now.

And very much like the kind of girl I was when I was with Hunter. I felt sick, sad, and embarrassed that I could draw a parallel between the asshole behavior Sebastian was describing and my own games with Hunter. "*Did* you love them? Any of them?"

"I loved the power I had over them. I loved that they loved me."

"That's not love. It's cruel." It was. I'd never gone that far with Hunter. Hunter had tried to push it that far, but I hadn't let him. I'd recognized who I became when I was with him, and I'd made it clear where we drew the line. I had stopped things before I'd really hurt him . . . because I couldn't stomach a happily ever after with someone like Hunter, not when being with him turned me into that version of myself.

"I know," Sebastian admitted. "I don't think I'm even capable of real love." He looked at me then, for the first time, and I could see that he looked frightened. "I'm afraid that I really *am* the guy everyone thinks I am." He paused, and I took his hand back in mine.

He continued, quietly. "My mom told my dad about what happened with Elizabeth—I mean, the whole thing blew up around me, and I missed a lot of classes, not to mention that most of my town knows she's pretty much on suicide watch now, thanks to scumbag Sebastian—and I've spent this whole fucking break trying to prove to my dad that I'm not that guy. That I'm not the kind of guy who treats a girl like shit. That I'm not the kind of guy who picks up girls everywhere I go and throws them away when I've finished with them."

He looked up at me with sad, disappointed eyes, and I wanted to touch his face—but surely that wouldn't help just now. Sebastian held my gaze. Studied my lips. "That's where you complicated things, Chaz. I started to fall for you, for real. I didn't plan this. I'm afraid to tell my dad that after everything that happened with Elizabeth and Sabrina and Jessie, here I am, hooking up with some random girl and starting it all up, all over again."

"So your next target is a three-toed girl?" I teased. It took some of the edge off, for a moment.

"Being with you . . . it makes me want to know you, makes me want to hold you and feel you and touch you in a way I never have wanted before. And that scares me."

Chills went up and down my body. I knew the smartest thing would be to walk away from Sebastian now. He was a commitmentphobe with a history of playing girls to the point of hating themselves.

But I knew, somehow, that it could be different with us.

That first night he'd come into Matt's, I hadn't thought about this as anything other than hooking up, but suddenly it seemed like maybe there could be something more. I was free around Sebastian. For the first time in a long time I wasn't thinking only of sex. I knew, somehow, that he and I were on common ground.

Neither of us knew what it meant to feel or actually be real with another person. But maybe we were each other's perfect testing grounds.

I sat up on my knees, my hands still twisted into his, and crawled over to him. As our lips connected, I pressed my body against his and pushed him down on the couch. Then I pulled away, and we looked at each other. He brought one of his hands up to my face and held my cheek, his thumb playing with my lip before he kissed me again.

A quiet fear washed over me then. I was suddenly overwhelmed by something unfamiliar and overpowering and a little bit dark. I put my head down against Sebastian's chest, with my body snuggled in against his side, and we lay there quietly for a long time, our bodies intertwined, just holding each other. My heart was racing.

His hand was on my stomach, his fingers tracing circles around my belly button. I put my hand on his chest and felt his heart leaping up to *thump-thump* under my palm. I turned my face up so I could kiss his chin, his cheek. I tickled his ear with my tongue, and he squeezed me tighter.

"Why are you still here?" Sebastian murmured, as I snuggled in against him.

I put my hand on his stomach, then snuck it under his shirt to feel the smooth path from his belly up to his chest. His skin was warm, but he had a trail of goose bumps running across his body in all the places I touched him. "Because I live here," I answered. "The question is, why are you still here?"

"You haven't kicked me out yet."

"And I don't plan to," I said. "You're keeping me warm."

"Is that it?"

"Yes, definitely." And then I kissed him again, and I was suddenly a lot hotter than I needed to be. I rolled onto my back, and somehow my shirt was off moments later.

Then Sebastian took his shirt off, and suddenly we were

skin to skin. He stopped kissing me just long enough to mur-mur, "Am I keeping you warm enough still?"

I answered by pushing against him, our bodies melting into each other. He flipped me over so I was under him, and I wrapped my legs around his. We were twisted up, and I was spinning, and I wanted him more than I'd ever wanted anyone before.

And then I stopped.

One minute we were making out and so close to doing everything I'd always wanted to do with a guy (but more than anyone, him) . . . and the next we were just holding each other again. Cuddled up, with Audrey Hepburn dancing and laugh-ing behind us on the TV. It felt so right, so perfect.

We lay there, cuddling and hugging for the rest of the movie, until it was over and Sebastian had to leave to get home for a late dinner with his dad. "Can I come over tomorrow?" he asked, as he put his shirt back on. I was propped up on my elbow on the couch, watching him get dressed with a big huge smile plastered across my face.

"Yes. I work until seven, though. Want to meet me at Matt's and we can get dinner?" I thought about that, and how it would put him right smack-dab in the middle of my life. He'd been to Matt's a million times before, but now that we'd had these afternoons together, it felt different and, somehow, more complicated—he'd be touching a very real part of my life, outside the comfort and security of our secluded afternoons together.

He nodded happily. "Okay," he said, then leaned down to give me one last perfect kiss.

Tomorrow couldn't come soon enough.

**20.** ■ **THE NEXT MORNING I WOKE UP LATE**

and went for a run. The snow had finally stopped overnight, and the plow had actually been pretty diligent about getting down my road after the accident on Christmas Eve. So I ran across the plowed section and found myself out on the main road, with a mental goal of making it to Sadie's house to check in on her.

When I jogged up, I could see her sitting in her kitchen, eating a yogurt. Her mom was sitting at the table across from her, and they were laughing about something on the other side of the room. When they let me in the back door, I realized Trav was standing by the sink. They were all just standing around the kitchen chuckling. "Hey," I said, breathless.

"Chastity," Sadie's mom said, offering me a glass of water. "Thank you so much for your help with Sadie's situation."

Huh? I looked at Sade, and she smiled at me. Trav was standing there beaming at me too. "No problem?" I offered, somewhat freaked out by the happy family dynamic they all had going on.

"Trav and I decided to tell our parents, Chaz," Sadie explained. "I realized I needed the support. After I told Trav about losing the baby, I just couldn't stop crying." Sadie's mom went over and wrapped an arm around her daughter's shoulder.

Even though I should have been thrilled that Sadie had such a strong support network, I was sort of sickened by the togetherness.

"I'm feeling a lot better now," she went on, "and we got in to see the doctor yesterday. Things look okay on the inside, and I'm starting to feel a little less depressed and disappointed."

I hugged her then, realizing that just because I didn't have the courage to tell anyone anything, I shouldn't be jealous that Sadie had the great family she did and was able to share her fears and sadness with people. While my arms were wrapped around her, Sadie whispered, "Do you want me to drive you home? We can talk."

I nodded, and after a couple of Christmas cookies and more of the supportive chitchat, I was in the car with my best friend—alone. While we drove out toward my house, Sadie told me about how she'd told Trav about losing the baby and how they'd decided—together—to bring their parents into the discussion. Her parents had only slightly freaked about the fact that they were having sex, and Sadie's mom even admitted that the pill might be a good idea. It seemed like Sade had really figured things out and was being healthy about working through her sadness and grief.

"I'm scared, Chaz." Sadie threw me off when she said this—listening to everything she was saying, it sounded like it was all fine and dandy and wrapped up with a bow. I guess it seemed like that to me, since we'd reached the point in the conversation where—if it had been me talking—I would have stopped, smiled, and promised her that everything was going great.

"What are you scared of?" I asked. "Everything sounds like it's right on track."

"I don't know what's going to happen with Trav," she admitted. "It's all been a lot to deal with. Too much. I feel like he's holding something back now—like we have this unspoken something that is sort of ripping us apart and making everything really weird. The baby sort of pulled us together somehow, and now that it's gone, it's like we're slipping apart."

She pulled into my driveway, and we sat next to each other, listening to the creaking sounds the car made while it cooled. "You'll get through it," I reassured her. "You always figure it out."

"Maybe not this time," she said, looking over at me. "I don't have everything figured out, you know." Sadie said this quietly, as if she knew it would startle me. "Things change."

I took her hand. This confession—the admission that the future wasn't all paved and mapped out and committed for my best friend—made me feel so much closer to Sadie than I ever had. She'd always been the one with the perfect family and the perfect boyfriend and the perfect future. But I recognized now, watching her face morph under the uncertainty of it all, that no one had that. It was stupid, really, but suddenly I felt like there was a whole new openness and connection between us. We were together in our uncertainty, and she was much more real to me now than she ever had been before. I knew I, too, could be more real for her.

After a few long moments of silence Sadie said, "What's

going on with you?" Her tone told me she wasn't just asking for a generic answer.

She followed me inside my house, and we sat in my room and talked. It all poured out of me—I told her everything that had happened with my parents and the accident, and about my unsent school applications and spilling the truth to my dad. I told her about Hunter and how I was a horrible bitch for rejecting the nicest guy in town who loved me for what I wasn't. Then, finally, I told her all about Sebastian.

I told her I thought I was falling in love with him, and when I said it to her, I knew I meant it. "So I guess I'm scared too," I admitted, more to myself than to her. "I've always talked such a big game, but when it really comes down to it, I'm scared of what he makes me feel. I'm scared of how vulnerable I feel around him, and I'm scared that he's leaving at the end of the week. I'm scared to let myself go and have it hurt later."

She listened patiently to everything, smiling when I was trying to make her laugh, and nodding when I talked about how things were with Sebastian. I loved how good I felt now that I'd said it all out loud.

I realized, as I told Sadie everything, that it was Sebastian who had started to turn the lock on something in me that was allowing me to open up, something that made me feel comfortable showing all the secret bits that don't always look so sexy. The emotional mess that is the equivalent of the unshaven, lumpy parts that only the people you really trust are invited to see (and they will love you afterward, no matter how weird and funny-shaped those parts are).

Sadie listened and hugged and supported, and I was so grateful for this opportunity to talk to my best friend without fear of her judging me and questioning my fucked-up logic. She was happy for me, truly happy. And then she started asking the questions. Eventually, she asked, "So, how far has it gone?"

"If you mean have we had sex—no."

"No?" She was clearly shocked. Then she looked suspicious. "What's wrong with him?"

I chewed my lip, which made me think about the way Sebastian watched my mouth as I was talking, and I couldn't wait for tonight. "It's different, Sadie. At first all I wanted to do was jump him. He was my chance to finally do it with someone other than Hunter Johnson." I paused, thinking about the night before. "But now there's so much more than just sex and making out and wanting to get some. There's this feeling, this *something*, that's making me less . . . I don't know . . . go-go-go or something. I just get so consumed with him, and it scares me to go there."

Sadie smiled, a slow, secret smile. "That's how it's supposed to be, Chaz." She beamed, as though I'd finally uncovered the meaning of sex and love and everything in between. "That's what making love is all about."

It was sweet, this declaration she made, but honestly, that wasn't it for me. I'd never believed the two necessarily had to go together. Sex and love could be separate things . . . but now that it looked like they *would* be together—or at least the foundation of love with the potential for sex—that's what was hanging me up. It was different, all of a sudden. Scary, somehow. I didn't say anything, but the way Sadie was shaking her head and rolling her eyes at me made it clear she knew we still had differing opinions on this. "Yeah, yeah, I know," she admitted.

My cell beeped then. I had a text from Angela. "Shit, Sade, I'm twenty minutes late for my shift. I still smell like sweat and feel totally disgusting. Will you hang out for a couple minutes while I shower and maybe drive me in to Matt's? That way I can get a ride home from Sebastian later."

Sadie laughed. "Of course I'll wait. My mom and Trav are probably still at my house bonding. I don't really want to go back there yet—it's all way too weird." She shuddered. "But you have to promise you'll comb your hair. If there's a chance you're going to finally get some real action tonight, I want you to look cute, okay?"

"Whatever you say," I said, pulling my shirt off as I ran to the shower.

"Yo, Chaz, girl." Vic hailed me from one of the booths in Angela's section, where he had been sitting with a hot blonde. The girl had just headed toward the ladies' room when Vic called over to me.

I wandered over, nodding at the girl's back. "Who's the eye candy, Vic?"

"That's my cousin, Erica, from Michigan. She's sweet, right?"

I chuckled, thinking about one of my first conversations with Sebastian. I wondered how many toes Vic had—his family probably had some interesting ancestry. "You're cute together."

"Yeah." He sighed. "I wouldn't mind tapping that."

"That's sick."

Vic's hands went up, defensive. "I didn't say I ever would. But she is a sweet piece of ass. Did I mention she's my *second* cousin?" He grinned. Just then Tina came breezing through the front door. She looked at Vic, then went straight up to the bar, where she laid a fat kiss on Danny Idol's mouth. Where the hell had that come from? *Someone got her Christmas wish. . . .*

Tina's eyes were open through the kiss, watching Vic.

He shrugged, rolling his eyes at me. "That doesn't bug you?" I asked. "He's Danny Idol, you know. Milton's hometown hero."

"Whatever. She's Tina Zander. That's my chick, no matter what Pretty Singing Boy thinks."

He looked weirdly unpissed, but I figured I'd better head off any trouble before it started. "If you're going to fight over her, can you take it outside? We have customers."

"I'm not gonna fight," Vic said, leaning back in his booth. "Not worth it. Especially since I know that as soon as the prom posters go up, she'll come running back to me, lips all puckered up and whiny." He switched to a high, falsetto, über-insulting "girl" voice. "Oh, Vic, my honey stud. Take me to prom! Please, please fuck me in my prom dress."

I just shook my head and walked away—Vic was laughing his ass off. He was crass, but at least he was honest. You couldn't fault him for that. He and Tina had something "special," that much was for sure.

Was it what I wanted? Not really.

But it was becoming increasingly impossible to figure out what I *did* want.

I knew I wanted Sebastian in the same raw, physical way I always had. But there was something else there that was making me look before I leaped.

I mean, sure, I still wanted sex. Sebastian was hot, and I hadn't changed my whole moral code in the last week and a half. But when I was with him, sex felt a lot more daunting because there was all this other emotional stuff packaged up with it. That was what I'd been thinking about all day, and what I was still thinking about when Sebastian came into Matt's at six thirty.

He took a seat at the bar and watched me delivering cheeseburgers to a table of snowmobilers. When I came back to the bar, unable to hold back my grin, his smile mirrored mine, and we both looked like fools falling in love. It made me laugh. When I did, he held out a finger, and I reached out across the bar to touch his finger with my own. Just a tiny little touch, nothing mind-blowing to any observer, but it rocked me to the core and sent shivers down my spine. "Mmmm," I murmured. "Hi. I'll be done in, like, half an hour?"

"I'll wait."

"You better." I grinned again, feeling even more like a love-struck puppy. I realized now why Angela and Sadie and Tina and all the other girls in town were always such saps when it came to guys. I was a fawning fool now too.

When Matt finally declared that I was cut a little after seven, I went after the open booth in the back and motioned for Sebastian to follow me. We passed Vic and his cousin on the way, and Vic whistled at me like I was some sort of pageant queen on parade. Then he grabbed my ass, and I expertly swatted his hand away. I looked back at Sebastian, and he was trying to hide a laugh.

We sat down, and he said, laughing out loud now, "The guys in this town have a lot of class, don't they?"

"Vic is unique," I explained. "We've had a little game going since junior high. That's his cousin, by the way . . ."

Sebastian laughed even harder. "Of course it is." When he stopped laughing, he started to say something, then stopped.

"What?" I asked.

"Nothing . . ." He looked bashful and sweet and unsure.

I took his hand and asked again, "What? You can ask me anything, you know. You've broken the seal of truth already."

"It's just . . ." He ducked his head, clearly embarrassed. Quietly, he said, "Have you been with a lot of guys?"

"That's what you wanted to ask?" I blurted out. "Seriously?"

"I'm sorry," he said. "I don't want to make you uncomfortable. I'm just wondering, since it seems like a lot of people are, you know, interested, and you . . ."

I laughed. He hadn't yet realized how open I was about this kind of thing. "You get that vibe, huh?"

"I don't know why it matters," he admitted. "I guess I just want to know. After I heard that guy Danny talking about you, and now that guy with the cousin, and the dorky guy your parents are hooking you up with . . . it just seems like I have some steep competition."

I giggled, totally girly and strange. "You don't have any competition," I admitted. "Trust me." I closed my eyes for a second, willing myself to be honest with him. "There aren't a lot of hot prospects in town, and I guess I'm still sort of a virgin. Not technically one hundred percent virgin, but in my estimation I'd call it eighty percent pure."

"Eighty percent pure?" That made him laugh again.

"I'm not proud of my stats, though."

He looked at me curiously. "You wish you were one hundred percent pure, right?" I was pretty sure he was being sarcastic, but I couldn't tell.

"Not quite," I said, realizing I sounded a little trampy without the context. "It's not that I'm eager to get it on with every guy that crosses my path, but I don't really feel this hyperactive urge to save myself for marriage."

He nodded, recognizing that I wasn't saying this as a come-on or making an announcement that he would definitely get in my pants. I knew that he knew we were just talking at this point—but that didn't mean I wasn't thinking about touching him later.

"The one thing I'm proud of," he said quietly, pausing for

a second when Matt delivered complimentary sodas to our table, "is that even though I've been a total jackass to every girl I've been with over the last . . . well, the last six years, I guess . . . I haven't slept with any one of them. I guess a part of me, deep down, knew that would be taking things a little too far. Sex and flee would make me a real asshole." He grimaced, and put his piece of gum in the corner of a napkin before taking a swig of his soda. "I've fucked with them emotionally, but at least I haven't fucked anyone over physically."

I listened silently, touching his hand lightly and quickly across the table. He continued, "My parents had me when my mom was still in high school. They were totally in love, and she got pregnant, and they decided to keep me—and things were great for about five years. And then the story goes that my dad slept with someone else, and my mom kicked him out, and he took off. He floated around for about ten years, trying to make it up to me and trying to redeem himself as a nonasshole in my mom's mind. And now, here I am, trying to redeem myself as a nonasshole with my dad. My mom has no faith in either of us, which is partly why I'm here with him now. I figured at least my dad and I could try to stick together."

I chewed my straw, watching him squirm under the weight of his story. "I don't know if it will help, but"—I paused, looking at him for a reaction—"you don't have to tell him about us."

He smiled. "Isn't it funny that I finally found a girl I feel great about, and you're telling me to hide you from my dad? If I could explain the way I felt about you in some sort of logical way, I would actually win some good-boy points."

"Something about keeping this covert and quiet and just between us makes me feel like we can't screw it up in the usual way. It's all a little more special, somehow." When I said that, I knew I meant it. I had no intention of telling my parents or Angela or anyone—except Sadie—just how much had happened with Sebastian. It was our little secret, and we'd see what happened. But keeping it private put so much less pressure on the outcome.

He nodded and smiled that slow, seductive grin, and I knew he got it. "You're unique, and strange, and beautiful," he murmured, tracing a heart across my lips with his thumb, and I just melted.

21.

AFTER WE ATE OUR BURGERS

(no onions) and said good-bye to Angela, Wolf, and the gang,
Sebastian drove me back to my house. For some reason I was
nervous as we drove up my driveway, and I almost passed out
thinking about him following me into the house.

I think he could tell I was a little off, because he wrapped
his arms around me as soon as we were through the front door
and buried his face in my (only slightly combed) hair. We stood
like that for a long while, him holding me and me letting him.

My parents were still in Minneapolis, were staying another

night and would be home tomorrow or the next day or sometime—I didn't really care. We had the house to ourselves for a while, at least, but even still, it felt weird having him here. I didn't like the way the lines between Sebastian and my regular life were starting to blur. I wanted to keep him in this little pocket of Christmas break, hidden from everything that had come before him. He was the best thing that had ever happened to me, and I wanted to keep that special somehow.

I suggested we load up some wood and late-night snacks and go out to the house in the woods. It was the one place that was uniquely ours right now, and somehow, leaving my house, leaving all the history behind, made the fairy tale we had going feel somewhat more complete.

Sebastian grabbed some blankets from the basement—he was getting smart about our winter weather (regardless of how foolish his wannabe coat from North Carolina was). We climbed on the back of the snowmobile, me wrapped around him this time, since Sebastian insisted on driving. "It makes me feel powerful," he explained. "Since I don't have the control with you, I need to get my passion for power out somehow. Let me drive? Please?"

His desperation made me smile, and I relented, happy to be hidden behind him on the snowmobile, with his back keeping me warm and my hands—mittens off—tucked up inside his jacket, touching his bare skin in the hidden places under his sweater. When we got out to the warming shack, it was just the same as we'd left it, though now it was bone cold and pitch black, with a faint hint of wood smoke from our fire there a few days before.

I got to work building a fire, while Sebastian set up a snuggly-looking nest on the floor. He lit the candles we'd thrown in at the last minute—totally romantic and totally cheesy, but the irony of it all made it somehow more acceptable. Neither of us was the romance-by-candlelight type, which was why it was all the more appropriate.

Once the fire was cooking, we sat on the floor, wrapped together in blankets, and continued the conversation we'd started at Matt's. I told him about my experiences with Hunter, and I talked about how bad I'd felt that I couldn't give him the relationship he was looking for. He told me more about Elizabeth, and how he had always tried to start a new relationship the healthy way, but that as soon as he kissed a girl, he knew it was all over. He knew he was going to break her heart.

"Is that how it is with me?" I asked, touching his lips with my own when he returned from loading the stove up with more wood. "Now that you've gotten your kiss, I'm out the door?"

"Yup," he said, wrapping his arm around my waist to twist me so we were lying together on the floor. He bunched up a piece of the blanket to make me a little pillow. "Absolutely." I laughed, and he kissed me gently. "Are you saying I have the power to tell you how this is going to end?" he asked, teasing. "I get to call the shots?"

"Um . . ." I pretended to think about it. "Maybe not. I think you've shown me you can't be trusted with a girl." I tucked in against his chest and felt his arms around me, begged the fire not to go out so we could stay here all night. "We can figure it out together," I said finally.

"I love that," he murmured. "Together."

And that's when I knew I was—without a doubt—starting to love him. I put my hand on his cheek and let it run across his chin, over to his ear. I played with his hair while he kissed me. I had never wanted someone so much, but it was a controlled kind of longing at first—not an urgent, immediate need. The kind of desire that you want to stretch out, anything to make it last as long as possible.

He touched my neck, and I shivered despite the fact that I was warm and comfortable. I let him trail his fingers down my neck and over my chest and stomach. He moved slowly, carefully, savoring every touch. When his hand got down to my hips, I held his hand in my own while we kissed, and I breathed in his cinnamon scent.

We touched and held each other for a long time—he had

to get up once to load the fire, and that's how I knew it must be the middle of the night. We'd gone through most of our wood, but I would rather have frozen to death than leave this night with him. Things progressed so naturally, so easily, that I hardly noticed we were both shirtless, our bodies touching each other, skin clinging as close as possible.

I wanted him so badly now. All I wanted was to feel him even closer to me, every part of him touching me. I guided his hand down my body and helped him open the button on his jeans. He looked up at me, his multicolored eyes searching mine, piercing into my heart. There was sadness and fear and hope and wanting. "Please," I whispered. "Trust me."

"I do," he said confidently, quietly. "It's me I'm worried about."

I smiled. "You'll be fine." I said this gently, with no intention of pushing him further than he was willing to go. "We're doing this together, right?" I kissed him again then, and the room spun away as he held me tightly and our arms wrapped around each other and I felt his hands touching my back and my stomach and reaching down to wrap my legs around him under the blankets.

It all felt so surreal—more powerful than I'd ever thought it could. He held me close, his body touching mine gently, carefully. We were both completely naked under the blankets now, and I didn't feel even the smallest bit of apprehension or fear. All my senses were heightened as we pressed into each other. I had brought condoms, and we struggled to get one on. His hands were shaking and fumbling, and I was laughing and crying all at the same time. "You're crying," he said, concern ringing through his voice.

"I know," I laughed. "Ignore that. It's a good thing." I helped him with the condom, and suddenly we were back under the covers, holding each other tightly, and he kissed me as we moved together.

It didn't hurt like I thought it would. Partly because he was being so gentle and slow about everything, careful to not finish before things had started, probably. It felt incredible to be so close to him, to share this experience with Sebastian. Neither of us really knew what we were doing, but I didn't care—I just wanted to stay there with him forever. It lasted a lot longer than I thought it would, and when it was over, he kissed my stomach and held my hand to his lips.

We slept like that for the rest of the night, his head against my belly, with my neck resting on the little pillow he'd made for me inside our nest.

"What's going to happen when you leave?" I asked the next morning. We had both woken up freezing when the sun came up and the fire had obviously run out of logs. I wasn't expecting a specific answer, and I wasn't even sure what the right answer was.

He put his cheek against mine, wrapping me up in that snuggly, warm, wonderful feeling, and held me against him. "I don't know," he said. "What do you want to happen?"

"I don't know," I admitted. We both laughed at the uncertainty of it all. "Thank you," I said suddenly.

"For what?" he asked, grinning. "For that mind-blowing sex?" He laughed.

"Yes, for that," I said, laughing too. We both knew there was room for improvement, but as far as *real* first times go, ours had been pretty amazing. Even though it wasn't a technical masterpiece (practice makes perfect, right?), the way I felt during and after certainly couldn't be beat. "I didn't think it would feel that . . . I don't know . . ." I broke off, at a loss for the right description.

"It just felt right, right?" he said, summing things up perfectly.

"Yeah, it just felt right." I grinned and sat up to kiss him again. While we loaded up the snowmobile and drove back to my house, I thought about how it was strange the way "right" could mean so many things. I had felt so emotionally connected and physically connected, and being with him felt right in every possible way. It all thrilled me. I thought about my conversation with Sadie and how she'd talked about sex being this emotional masterpiece; I'd scoffed, but in this case, she had been right.

And that was all right by me.

His flight was booked for New Year's Eve. Less than four full days and Sebastian would be gone. I felt a little silly admitting this, even just to myself, but I knew he'd be taking a piece of me with him. But more importantly, he would be leaving me with a much bigger piece of myself than had existed before he'd ever come.

As I thought about this, and wondered how soon was too soon for me to be with him again (an hour? four?), I walked into my house to take a shower and possibly a nap. I found my mom in the living room. The house had been mostly empty since Christmas Eve, and I was surprised at how happy I was to see her home.

Cold air blew in with me, and Mom looked up from her place on the couch. I could see she'd been crying, and her face was broken and scared. It was alarming to see my mom like this, and I didn't know what to say. I just looked at her, and she looked back at me, and we said nothing. Until, finally, I walked toward her and put my hand on her shoulder. "Are you okay, Mom?"

"Fine," she said cheerfully, waving her hand in the air to brush me off. "Were you at Sadie's, honey? Have they been taking good care of you?"

"Yeah." The lie came out easily. "Mom, please . . . what's wrong? Is it Dad?"

"Your dad is fine. He's officially obese, according to the BMI chart, but we all knew that already." She smiled, trying hard to make light of her emotions and the fear. I recognized what she was doing—I was an expert at what she was doing too—but I wanted her to open up to me. I wanted to see what was behind the curtain. I wanted to know my mom. "We'll get through the cancer, you know." She said this for herself more than for me—I realized it was the first time she'd brought up the cancer without me forcing it.

I nodded. "Then what is it?" I pried, begging her with my eyes to let me in. When she said nothing, just hid her eyes from me, I quietly admitted, "Mom, I'm freaked out too."

She tilted her head, and for a moment it looked like we might actually see each other as people. And then she stood up and brushed off her pants, smoothing out unseen wrinkles and brushing off invisible lint. "Yes, well . . ." She smiled thinly, sadly. "We'll be just fine." She patted my arm, then looked at me quizzically. "Do you need me to order more of that shampoo? Your hair looks a mess."

I didn't know what to say. It wasn't going to be easy for us—she'd spent forty-some years perfecting the impenetrability of her candy shell. I knew that, like me, Mom probably had something gooey and good inside, but I didn't know if she'd ever be willing to share it. I drew some comfort from the fact that I could see less of myself reflected in her than I would have if I'd really looked even just a few days before. I had a long way to go, and an uncertain future that scared the hell out of me, but at least I could admit that.

I wondered if my mom had anyone she could be honest with. I wondered if she was even honest with herself. I couldn't change her, but I could change me, and that would have to be enough.

22. **I HAD TO WAIT A FULL TWENTY-FOUR**

hours to see Sebastian again. A last-minute extra shift at Matt's—complete with what felt like a full hour of watching Angela and Ryan make out next to the fryer, which was probably why Matt needed the extra help—followed by a belated night of opening Christmas gifts with my parents was pure torture when I knew what I could be doing. When I knew we only had a few days left and then . . . ?

It was funny, really, to see how whipped I was. As I sat around the "It looks so real!" Christmas tree in our living room (festooned with small Swedish flags and those damn crocheted elves), I pretended to be emotionally present. My mind was with Sebastian while I opened a gift box containing a heinous holiday sweater and a second box with a less heinous pair of running pants.

My last gift was a wrapped copy of that book about college I'd been paging through when I went shopping with Sadie before Christmas. I already knew how the book ended—with no answers for me—and hoped the store would be willing to accept a return without the receipt. My dad glanced at me when I opened the book, saying nothing, but his look was priceless. He knew I had a difficult conversation in store with my mom after New Year's, and his amused expression told me he had no intention of helping me get through it.

"I swung by the admissions office while we were down at the U yesterday." My mom singsonged this as she unwrapped one of her gifts—a songbook entitled *Holiday Harvest!* My dad pretended to have this serious look on his face (even though he was grinning wildly every time she wasn't looking at him) and kept nodding when my mom gestured for backup. "They weren't willing to *directly* discuss the status of your application, but I got the sense they recognized your name when I mentioned it. I bet you'll get your acceptance letter any day now!"

I nodded somberly. "If it comes soon, it will be a true Christmas miracle."

My mom bowed her head. "Amen to that."

Dad popped a meatball in his mouth to keep from laughing. Emotionally, my mom and I were miles farther from each other than I think we'd ever been, but at least Dad and I had found a comfortable place—not a close-up, snuggly place, but something that made us feel somewhat connected. "The meatballs are good," he said, helping me change the subject through a mouthful of beef and venison. "The deer really adds something to 'em."

Mom swatted his shoulder playfully. "Dan, you didn't!" She almost sounded flirty. It was freaky.

"I'll bite . . . didn't what?" I asked, mildly concerned.

"Put the roadkill in the meatballs." Dad shrugged. "I didn't want the Johnsons to smoke the whole thing—venison's worth something these days. You pay a high price for fresh deer meat. There are already piles of rock-hard jerky in the Johnsons' shed—it had to stop." He laughed.

My mom tittered along with him—maybe she wasn't as sterile as I thought. Maybe I'd been so busy paying attention to how she interacted with me—and how I interacted *like* her—that I had failed to notice how she related to my dad. Maybe, like me with Sebastian, my dad opened her up somehow. *Um, ew.* Also, unlikely.

"When do you get your stitches out, Dad?" My dad's stitches tore a dark gash across the top of his forehead, which was noticeable when he took off the winter hat I'd given him as a gift. Now he was opening my second gift—a seat belt cushion wrap that would make the belt more comfortable across his midsection. I hoped he would take the hint and start wearing it.

Dad smiled at the gift, then said, "I'm going to have one of the nurses down at the U take them out when I'm there later this week. We were able to get in another round of sessions with the researchers, and I have some treatments scheduled. Quite the way to ring in the New Year."

"I thought the cancer hasn't spread?" I probed. Here I was, back in the dark with no details again. At least it sounded like I'd have the house to myself for a few more days. "Aren't you done at the U?"

Dad nodded. "I agreed to be a part of this research group. A lot of the treatments will be provided free of charge since I'm part of a medical study—I just have to keep going for a few months. The bank's medical insurance isn't great, and with me only working part-time—"

"But your dad is just fine." Mom smiled at me, reassuring no one. "No biggie. Who wants *kladdkaka*?"

"I want to talk about it like a normal family, Mom." I said

this levelly, and I looked her in the eye. "Serving cake won't cure the cancer."

"Neither will talking about it," she spat back. I knew exactly how she felt, but for the first time I didn't feel the same.

"This impacts all of us, the whole family," I said, giving her a look that I knew would push her further than I had that morning. She turned away from me, her eyes filling with tears again, before skulking off to the kitchen to cut pieces of cake.

My dad looked wildly uncomfortable and followed after her. It was then that I realized with absolute certainty that I would never be one of those people who would go off into the world and then turn toward home to find a place where I could feel like myself again. I'm not a Lifetime movie with the happy family ending and the very merry Christmases around a plastic tree. As it turns out, home isn't ever going to be where my heart is.

I've always known I need to direct my own future so I don't risk ending up like my mom. I don't want her future—I want something more for myself than an emotionally constipated existence where fear and longing are like four-letter words.

I want to feel and be like the person I am when I'm with Sebastian.

And *that* is why the future—its unplanned uncertainty—excites and scares the hell out of me.

*　　*　　*

When it came to sex with Sebastian, "practice makes perfect" definitely rang true.

It's not that sex was all we were doing in our last few days together—we spent hours lying around and talking and going for walks in the snow and just *being* together. But we also fit in a bit more practice on the whole sex thing, and I was definitely starting to get the hang of it. I felt alive and energized and totally, completely in love.

"What are your thoughts on asparagus?" he asked me out of the blue two days after my family's Christmas celebration. We were lying on his bed after an impressive make-out session. I'd been at his house all morning, since ten minutes after his dad had left for work, and I was planning on staying until he kicked me out.

"Stinky pee," I responded, twisting his hair into little curls.

He swatted my hand away playfully, and I sat, straddling him, on his stomach. "Does it bother you that your town only has one nonwhite family?"

"I've never really thought about it. . . ." I pondered this while I leaned over to braid a piece of my hair into his. Milton is overwhelmingly Caucasian. "It doesn't bother me, but it is intriguing."

"Simon and Garfunkel or the Rolling Stones?"

"Janis Joplin."

"Of course," he laughed. "A headstrong female." In between experimentation with sex and an unresolved discussion about each of our futures, we had spent hours on a game Sebastian liked to call First Date. Questions that were simple to answer, and that helped distract us from the overwhelming realization that we had less than a day left together before New Year's Eve, the day Sebastian would be going home.

I had learned that he disliked mushrooms, had a strange fascination with the taste of blood, and had once kissed a real frog on a dare.

"You love a headstrong female too." I tickled him under the chin, and he pulled me down to lie on top of him.

"I do," he whispered, and we promptly ditched First Date in order to snuggle under the covers. He pushed my shirt up and off and kissed my navel tenderly. He kept touching kisses to my belly, until his hands wandered downward to my thighs and his mouth found my hips. I tensed up until Sebastian looked up, and our eyes locked.

Then he smiled at me in his seductive, mouthwatering way, and I was nothing more than jelly.

Later that night, long after most everyone else in Minnesota had gone to bed, Sebastian came over—telling his dad he was going to a party with some of the locals he'd met over break—and we were together for the last time.

We lay next to each other on the floor, like we had the first night we'd been together, and held each other tight. "I never even thought myself capable of this level of cheesiness," I admitted, flipping on to my side to face him, head resting on palm.

"And I never thought I'd eat meat again."

I looked at him curiously, thinking of all the cheeseburgers he'd eaten at Matt's over the last few weeks. And the venison jerky. "Huh?"

"Oh," he said, grinning. "Didn't I tell you I was a vegetarian before I got to Minnesota?"

I shook my head. "Uh, no. You don't act like much of a vegetarian. Burgers, jerky . . . Since when are you vegetarian?"

"For about five years—that's why that first burger you served me was so freaking delicious." He sighed hugely. "*So* delicious."

"You," I declared, pressing my lips to his mouth, "are a very naughty vegetarian."

He kissed me back, talking through the kiss. "And *you* are a pusher."

"I am not!" I laughed. "I had no idea. . . . If you had told me about your dietary restrictions, I would have brought you a dried-up, freezer-burned veggie burger or something."

"And it wouldn't have been nearly as good. I wanted the real thing, Chaz."

I smiled. "You definitely got that."

"I'm going to miss you," he blurted out suddenly, his eyes flickering from my eyes to my mouth and back again. "Can't I take you with me?"

"I'm going to miss you, too," I said sadly, taking his hand in my own. We had decided—together—that we wouldn't hold on. That tonight was the end of it. For now at least. Our time together was magical and captured perfectly in a moment in time, just steps outside the lines of our normal lives and held safely within a special exception space. A space that would hopefully sneak and creep and tiptoe into our normal lives and make both of us better people somehow. I knew that because of him I would actually exist in my life now.

Being with Sebastian, learning to feel and touch and just *be*—be *right* in the moment—had given me the confidence and clarity to know that I didn't need to have all the answers about my future. I didn't know when I would figure out what I wanted with the next year or the next fifty, but at least I could admit that the uncertainty scared me and thrilled me. And he'd snuck in and tilted this little piece of my life just enough that everything had changed.

As he kissed me once more, the spice of his cinnamon gum

penetrating every open space in my body, I considered the fact that Sebastian had shown me that I *could* have what I wanted and that I deserved to truly *want* what I could get. That I don't need to settle for passionless sex or boring romance. The two can be packaged together into something perfect—even when you aren't looking for it—and when it happens, it's scary and hot and fucking amazing.

EPILOGUE

WHEN THE CLOCK STRUCK MIDNIGHT,
and everyone at Matt's threw their arms in the air to celebrate
the arrival of the New Year, I watched my friends and thought
about Sebastian again. My fingers wrapped around the stick of
cinnamon gum in my pocket.

*He's probably all the way back to North Carolina now,
and I am here. Maybe we'll be together again; maybe we
won't. . . .* Long-term love and a storybook ending had never
been the planned outcome of our little romance.

Thanks to him, I know that beneath my sex-hungry veneer,

I am capable of love. And I'm certain there's a whole world of sex and love and everything in between out there, just waiting for me, and I'm ready to go out and find it. Whatever "it" might be.

So kiss it, fairy-tale endings. This story ended my way, and it is just the beginning.

ACKNOWLEDGMENTS

THIS BOOK WOULD NEVER HAVE COME TO BE WITHOUT Anica Rissi, phenomenal editor, collaborator, and all-around fun chick. Thanks for cupcakes and your courage.

Thanks also to designer Cara Petrus and her creative brilliance—you helped shape this story by sharing your inspiring vision for the cover before Chaz ever even existed.

The whole team at Simon Pulse simply rocks. I adore Bethany Buck, Jennifer Klonsky, Mara Anastas, Emilia Rhodes, the eternally positive Victor Iannone, and everyone else who makes Pulse so very fantastic.

A virtual box of brownies goes to Robin Wasserman and Jennifer Echols, both of whom read ugly and incomplete versions of this novel and offered support and sound advice throughout.

And, as always, I am immensely grateful for the support of my family and friends, who all suffered my mood swings while I wrote this book. Not to be dramatic, but Greg, you save my life a little every day with your patience and calming qualities. Hugs for being the right guy for me.

ABOUT THE AUTHOR

ERIN DOWNING STILL CAN'T FIGURE OUT WHAT SHE WANTS to do with her life (and probably never will), but she's living a pretty awesome one while she sorts it all out. A native of Duluth, Minnesota, Erin lived in England, Sweden, and New York City before settling down in Minneapolis with her husband and three kids. She is the author of three other teen novels—*Drive Me Crazy*, *Prom Crashers*, and *Dancing Queen*—as well as one middle-grade novel, *Juicy Gossip*. None of those books is anything like *Kiss It*, and that's what made writing this novel so much fun. She's currently working on her next novel for teens. Visit Erin on the web at www.erindowning.com.

Girls you like.
Emotions you know.
Outcomes that make you think.

ALL BY

DEBCALETTI

Friendship.

BETRAYAL.

Makeovers.

REVENGE.

And don't miss this other funny read from
Eileen Cook:

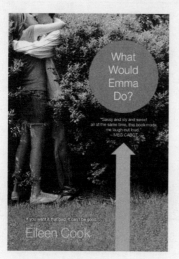

"Sassy and sly and
sweet all at the same time."
—Meg Cabot

From Simon Pulse • Published by Simon & Schuster

Which will be *your* first?

FROM SIMON PULSE

PUBLISHED BY SIMON & SCHUSTER

SimonTeen

Simon & Schuster's **Simon Teen**
e-newsletter delivers current updates on
the hottest titles, exciting sweepstakes, and
exclusive content from your favorite authors.

Visit **TEEN.SimonandSchuster.com** to
sign up, post your thoughts, and find out what
every avid reader is talking about!

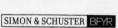